THE
TRIUMPH
OF EVIL

LAWRENCE
BLOCK

THE
TRIUMPH
OF EVIL

A FOUL PLAY PRESS BOOK
The Countryman Press
Woodstock, Vermont

Copyright © 1971 by Paul Kavanagh
This book originally appeared under the pseudonym
    Paul Kavanagh.
ISBN 0-88150-066-6
This edition is published in 1986 by Foul Play Press, a division
    of The Countryman Press, Woodstock, Vermont 05091.
Printed in the United States of America at Capital City Press

"Talk in French when you don't
know the English for a thing,
turn out your toes as you walk,
and remember who you are."
—THE RED QUEEN

"All that is required for the
triumph of evil is for good men
to do something wrong."
—MILES DORN

THE TRIUMPH OF EVIL

ONE

When the doorbell rang,

he was sitting at the kitchen table drinking tea and watching baby birds. A pair of robins had nested in the eaves over the kitchen window. The eggs had hatched a week ago, and since then he had found himself spending hours at a time watching them. There was little drama in it, no cuckoo egg in the robins' nest, no cats to be warded off, only the constant feeding and attendance by the parent birds and the steady growth and development of the young.

He set his cup down and went to the door, thinking that it would be the girl. "You're early," he said, drawing the door open.

There were two men on the step, and the taller man's brow wrinkled at Dorn's words. "Then you expected us?"

"No."

"You are Mr. Dorn? Miles Dorn?"

"Yes."

"And you are expecting someone?"

"In an hour, perhaps."

1

"Then we have time for a conversation," the taller man said. "May we come in?"

"Of course."

He led them to the living room. The two sat on opposite ends of his couch, an empty cushion between them. Above and between their heads was a framed print, an English fox-hunting scene. It had been there when he took the house, and although it was not to his taste he had decided against removing it. He liked its incongruity—this shabby southern town, this squat house of concrete block and stucco with its motel furniture and plasterboard walls, and this glorified representation of the unspeakable in pursuit of the inedible.

The smaller man lit a cigarette, and Dorn caught the odor of Turkish leaf. It triggered memories. Once all cigarettes had smelled thus.

The taller man said, "You were not expecting us; yet if our presence surprises you, you hide it well."

"I am rarely surprised." He wondered about the man's accent. It was slight, and had echoes of no particular place, as if this man, like Dorn, had had frequent changes of nationality. The man had a broad forehead, dark brown hair slicked down, heavy brows, large nostrils, a dark and somewhat oily complexion. The smaller man, who had not yet spoken, looked at once Latin and Oriental, and yet was almost certainly not a Cuban Chinese. Dorn thought it likely that these men would have something to do with Cuba and hoped he was wrong. The smaller man had very precise features and flat dark eyes and small hands. Dorn had learned that men of this sort were usually quite good with knives.

"You expect the unexpected," the tall man said.

"In a sense."

"It was not overly difficult to find you. This is a pleasant town. Trees and flowers. Well-kept lawns. Children playing in the streets. Do you own this house?"

"I rent it."

"I'm sure you're happy here."

"I've become comfortable."

"It's a common dream, don't you think? A house of one's own on a quiet street in a sleepy town. But dreams. Like smoke, easy to perceive and difficult to grasp firmly."

"I do have an appointment."

2

"Of course. It is your time that I am wasting, and I apologize. You will want to know who we are. My name is Vanders, Leopold Vanders. This is my associate, Mr. Robert Brown."

"My pleasure."

"Ours as well. But more than pleasure, I think, for all of us. We have something for you, Mr. Dorn."

His eyes stayed on Vanders but he concentrated on the smaller man, Brown, studying him out of the corner of his eye, looking for any sign of tension. If they meant to kill him, it would be Brown who would do the killing. He did not bother to wonder why they might want to kill him. Too many people had reasons of varying degrees of urgency. Dorn kept his eyes on Vanders and let his mind work out what his body would do if Brown moved or changed expression. Brown was at least ten and probably fifteen years younger than Dorn, presumably armed, and apparently in good condition. If they meant to kill him, Dorn thought, they would very likely succeed.

"A piece of work," Vanders said.

"I've retired."

"Do any of us ever really retire? I often wonder this myself. Dreams, you know. And smoke."

"What do you want of me?"

"You'll travel some. Meet with some people, assist in some arrangements. There's a project planned. Nothing unlike things you've done over the years."

"I'm not really interested."

"There's a bit of money in it for you. A thousand now, just for a handshake. And more to come. A good deal more if things go well enough. A fair sum even if they don't."

"I have no need of money just now."

"You could judge that better than I. My understanding is otherwise."

"I'm afraid I'm not interested," he said again. "And if I were—"

"Yes?"

"I don't know who you are."

Vanders nodded. "A problem. I could show you my driver's license or a letter of reference from my pastor, but that wouldn't be much help, would it? I might mention some names."

"Oh?"

"James Travis. Erno Vacek. Miller Harris." These were names

3

Dorn had used at one time or another. Vanders studied Dorn's face and looked disappointed. "You are unimpressed?"

"I assumed you knew something about me. I haven't been Miles Dorn long enough for you to come looking for me únder that name."

"Hans Neumann, then."

"Then you know a great deal about me. Still—"

"Other names. I might mention Gregorio Santresca, for example."

"What about Santresca?"

"Does he know where you are? And would you want him to?"

Dorn considered this. "I don't think he cares much. Santresca could probably find me himself if he wanted to. Why would he want to?"

"To kill you."

"Of course, but why?"

"To even a score."

"He has cause, I suppose. But if his mind works that way he has a long list, and I'd be nowhere near the top of it." He got to his feet. "I don't mean to be impolite, Mr. Vanders, Mr. Brown, but I am expecting someone. As you know. And I know nothing about you, I still know nothing about you, and I am not looking for work at the present time."

"You've retired."

"Exactly."

"There is a letter. A letter for you. Robert has it. You might want to read it."

Brown took the letter from his inside jacket pocket. He handed it carefully to Dorn, as if it were very important that the letter not be wrinkled. Dorn unfolded it. A dozen lines, handwritten on the letterhead of a Holiday Inn in Tampa.

He read it through twice and looked up, faintly puzzled. "All of this—money, names, veiled threats and allusions. All of that foolishness when you had something so much more persuasive at your disposal. I am assuming that this is genuine."

"Of course."

"And not written under duress. And that I could verify it with no difficulty."

"Of course."

"And yet you chose to hold it in reserve."

"Not exactly." Vanders smiled. It was a more open smile than

4

Dorn had had from him. "You might regard the offers and threats as a test. If they had moved you, you would never have seen the letter or heard from us again. You understand? If money could buy you or threats coerce you, you would not be right for our purposes." A flash of the smile again. "We only want that which it is most difficult for us to have. Some men strike this attitude with women."

"Or with almost anything."

"Yes."

He considered. "If Heidigger is a part of this, that does change things. In a fundamental way. Still—"

"Yes?"

"As I told you. I have retired. I haven't wanted work. I haven't wanted . . . that sort of life."

"And you are comfortable here?"

"Yes, I am."

"I wonder, though," Vanders said. "I wonder how much a man can decide whether or not he wants the sort of life that has been his. There is a saying to the effect that a man may change his shoes but must walk forever upon the same two feet. How much can we change ourselves, do you suppose? It is an interesting question."

"I have thought often about it. Quite often."

"It takes long thought."

Brown lit another cigarette. Dorn felt an unaccustomed longing for tobacco. He had given it up almost two years earlier on a doctor's advice, and couldn't recall the last time he'd felt such an urgent craving for a cigarette. It amused him.

"This piece of work," he said. "It would help to know more about it."

"What I said earlier was true enough. The work would be similar enough to things you've done before. What would be involved, really, would be not so much a single act or action as an ongoing association. There is a country that might be inclined to change its government. It is easier, I think, for a country to change its government than for a man to change his life."

"Is there CIA involvement?"

"In a sense. A community of interests on the part of some Agency people. You could call it that. Certainly nothing official. I believe you've worked with them in the past."

"And at cross-purposes, on occasion."

5

"It wouldn't be a factor."

"Perhaps not." He thought for a moment. "I presume you wish an answer, and that there is some sort of time factor involved. When would all of this begin?"

"Tomorrow."

"That soon."

"You would talk to Heidigger tomorrow. As far as when your particular role would turn active, I couldn't say."

"Yes. I would have to think about this."

"Understandable."

"I have no phone. If I could reach you perhaps this evening."

"We will be in transit, unfortunately. But there is a number you could call at nine-thirty tonight." He took a blank memo slip from a leather case and uncapped a fountain pen and jotted down a number from memory. He waved the slip so that the ink could dry before handing it to Dorn. The numbers looked European, and the seven was crossed.

"The line is presumably untapped, but we take the usual precautions as a matter of course. Please call collect. As close to nine-thirty as possible."

"What name shall I use?"

"Mine will do."

"Leopold Vanders."

"Yes." The two stood up abruptly, as if in response to a subtle signal. "I believe that's all. Please call, wherever your thinking leads you. And I hope you'll decide affirmatively. There is something I respond to in you. We could probably exchange some absorbing stories, you and I. Not that we ever will, but the capacity exists."

As they reached the door, Dorn said, "The country in question wouldn't be Cuba, would it? Because I wouldn't want to be involved if it were Cuba. I really can't work with those people."

"No. Nor I, if it comes to that. Obviously I can't tell you the country, but it's not Cuba."

"I suppose I would guess Haiti, if I were guessing."

"You ought to be allowed one guess. Not Haiti. A more substantial country than Haiti, I would say. And that, actually, is all I will say. Good-day, Mr. Dorn."

"Mr. Vanders. Mr. Brown."

Their car was at the curb, a late Ford station wagon with

Florida plates. Brown drove. Dorn watched the car disappear from view. He looked at his watch. She was late, which was as well. Just a few minutes late so far. He thought of canceling her lesson. Did he want company or solitude right now? It was hard to say.

Neither Cuba nor Haiti. It could, he decided, be any place at all. Africa, South America. He read a local newspaper on an infrequent basis and made no attempt to keep up with things. Not that this sort of affair would likely be predictable through published news stories.

Did no one retire? Was it so impossible to change one's feet, so futile to change one's shoes?

He had fresh tea made when she rang the doorbell. How fresh she looked, he thought, as he often did. How young, how untroubled.

"I almost didn't come," she said.

"Then I should have had to drink both cups of tea."

"I can't have a lesson, really. I mean, I can't pay you. Not today, at least. I'll probably have the money next week, and I could pay you then, but I can't be positive, see."

"It doesn't matter. Come in the kitchen, see my baby birds."

"Oh, yes," she said. "I was thinking about them the other day. They're all right?"

"They seem to be."

She sipped at her tea after exclaiming over the birds. "Oh, it's peppermint," she said.

"Spearmint, actually." And then in German, "I found it growing in the yard. It makes nice tea, don't you think?"

They went on talking idly in German. She had a surprising facility for the language, doubly surprising in that she seemed quite without motivation for learning it. She was his only pupil, one of three who had responded to a note he'd hung on the bulletin board at the Student Union. The other two were young men, both interested in learning French as preparation for a year at a French university. He had given them several lessons each before discovering that the lessons bored him immeasurably. Since he had undertaken them as an antidote to boredom, there was little point in continuing them.

But when Jocelyn came, there was an immediate mutual sense of mental stimulation. She was planning no junior year in Cologne or Munich. Indeed, she had already dropped out of the university and continued to live in town and spend time on the campus only because there was nothing else she cared to do.

"I would like to learn a language," she had told him. "Only I can't decide which one. French, German, Spanish, Serbo-Croat. Was Russian on the list, too? I can't remember."

"Yes, Russian also."

"I think it would be sensational to know Serbo-Croat, but what would I do with it? I don't suppose I could ever find anyone to talk to."

"Only in Yugoslavia."

"Is that where you're from?"

"Yes, from Croatia."

"How do you pronounce your first name? Is it Anglicized or what?"

"It was originally Mee-lesh. There was a diacritic mark over the s. But I pronounce it Miles. It's simpler for everyone, and after all this town is rather far from Croatia."

"Miles from Croatia. What language should I learn? What language would you most enjoy teaching?"

He told her it ought to be one she liked the sound of, and spoke paragraphs of each. In the other languages he said nothing significant, but in German he found himself saying, "You have spun gold for hair and pink cream for skin. Were I not beyond such things I would lift your skirt and spend hours kissing your pudenda."

After she had selected German and had a first lesson, he found himself wondering at his words. Such private jokes were not usual behavior for him.

In the months that followed he found himself taking increasing pleasure in the time they spent together. She came once a week at the start, then increased to Tuesdays and Fridays. Although the lessons were theoretically to last an hour, she generally stayed the full afternoon. He charged her five dollars a lesson. He would have been happy to forgo payment—ten dollars a week was an expense to her, and of no importance to him—but he had been careful not to suggest this lest it alter the structure of their relationship. She was the only friend in his present life and he did not want to do anything that might deprive him of that friendship.

Her facility with German impressed him. She retained vocabulary easily and had a remarkably good accent. A Prussian might

8

have been as apt to take her for a Swabian, perhaps, as for an American.

"I may not be staying here much longer," she said at one point. "I don't know." She switched abruptly to English. "The thing is, my father found out that I dropped out."

"You hadn't told him?"

"No. I suppose I should have, but somehow I couldn't get around to it. We don't communicate very well. We did once, I think, but something happened to us. It's funny, the way things happen to people."

"Was he very upset?"

"I'm not sure. I talked to him on the phone. Just last night, as a matter of fact. He went right into the heavy father number, but I think that may have been just a reflex. *Der gross Vater.* It doesn't translate, does it? It just means grandfather. Both of my grandfathers are dead. I have one grandmother living. I'm sure I told you that."

She had told him many things about herself—age, family background, childhood experiences. He told her about different places he had been without disclosing much about the person he had been while in those places. It was a special sort of conversation, the information serving primarily as vehicle for the words and phrases themselves. One could not pass hours chatting about an aunt's pen on an uncle's table. She spoke of classes and boyfriends and movies and things she had done as a child. She lived in Connecticut. Her father manufactured beads for dress manufacturers. Her mother was secretary-treasurer of the local chapter of the League of Women Voters, and had collected funds for Biafran relief. She had a brother in high school. A sister two years older than she had drowned seven years ago at Cape Cod. She had had a dog for several years in Connecticut. Now she had a cat named Vertigo. She often talked about the cat and had several times said she might bring it to Dorn's house. She had never done so.

On one occasion Dorn told her of a town in Slovenia where he had spent a day and two nights twenty-five years ago. He described the town and talked about the Slovene language and the local architecture. He told her of the meals he had eaten there, and of the wine, which was good but extremely tart. He did not tell her that he and two other men had gone to the burgomaster's house

9

in the middle of the second night. They searched the house but could not find the man. They knew he was there. Dorn held the wife's arms while a man named Gotter hit her in the breasts and belly with his fists. She wept but insisted her husband was not home. Dorn went into one of the bedrooms where a child had been sleeping. He brought the little boy out and told the woman he would put out the boy's eyes. It wasn't necessary to do this. The burgomaster was in a steamer trunk in the cellar. They had seen the trunk earlier but had not thought to open it—it looked too small to hold a man and the lock was rusted. They smashed the lock and took the burgomaster out of the trunk. He was a small plump man who wept soundlessly until Dorn shot him in the center of the forehead. They left immediately. Gotter wanted to rape the wife—the widow. Violent death acted as a sexual stimulant upon him. Dorn was never able to understand this. But on that occasion there was simply no time, and Gotter was disciplined enough to repress his lust.

Now Jocelyn was saying that she might go to Washington for the weekend. "There's a demonstration," she said in German, not having to hesitate for the noun. "Friends of mine are driving up, and I might go with them."

"A peace demonstration?"

"A memorial for Landon Waring."

"He was killed?"

"It was all over yesterday's paper, and on the radio all the time."

"I haven't seen a paper in several days. He was what? A Black Panther?"

"I'm not sure whether he was a Panther or just worked with them. He was in Jacksonville for a rally. Why would he come to the South? It seems so suicidal. The Gestapo killed him. Isn't that funny—we call them that, the police, but in the middle of a conversation in German."

"The police killed him?"

"The official lie is that he was trying to escape, and that he grabbed a pig's gun." Back to English. "I can't see how that could possibly go down with anyone. Even the Silent Majority has to know better than to believe it. He was a beautiful man, you know. I saw him speak once. Everybody's being killed. The kids I know, we were talking, and there's all this paranoia. Like it's a conspiracy. I don't know if it is or if it's just the way the whole country is going in two different directions, and each side hates the other side. There was a riot in Jacksonville last night. They had the National Guard. First the Gestapo and then the Brownshirts. I don't know, I just don't know. You want to do something, but you wonder what's the point, what good will it do. Like what good does it do to put one more body in Washington when no one pays any attention anyway. What good does it do."

"I don't think you should go."

"Why do you say that?"

He smiled. "For selfish reasons. Landon Waring is just a name to me, and a dead man's name in the bargain. You are a friend. It could be dangerous for you, and to no purpose."

"They can't kill everybody."

"No, of course not."

"Sometimes I feel guilty because I didn't go to Chicago. Of course I was only seventeen but I could have gone, some friends of mine did go. Nothing happened to them. The guilt—I don't feel guilty because I didn't go, but because I'm secretly glad that I didn't go. If that makes any sense. Sometimes I wonder what Megan would be doing now. She would be twenty-one, but she's fourteen forever now, and there's no way to guess who she would have grown into. She was always two years older than me and now she's frozen at fourteen while I get older and older. That's how death takes people away from you. It steals the people they would have been." She gave her head a sudden shake. "I'm sorry, Miles. This is terrible. I was very down last night and I keep slipping back into it. Let's talk about something else. I don't know what. The baby robins? Anything."

Not long before she left, she said, "What's that smell? I keep noticing it."

He had to consider. "Oh. A Turkish cigarette."

"You haven't started smoking?"

"No. I had a visitor earlier today."

"A student?"

She didn't know he had no other pupils. "Not a student," he said. "He smoked I think two cigarettes. The smell of Turkish leaf lingers."

"At first I thought it was grass."

11

"Marijuana?"

She nodded, and he laughed at the thought.

"You've never tried it?"

"Oh, no, no. I don't even drink coffee. A glass of wine at dinner, that's all."

"And spearmint tea."

"And spearmint tea."

"Maybe you should try it, someday."

"You use it?"

"Sometimes. Not often. So many people like to be high all the time." She caught her knee with her folded hands. Her expression turned impish. "I could turn you on," she said. "If you ever wanted."

"Don't you suppose I'm too old for that?"

"You never seem old to me."

There was something hard to read in her eyes. He shifted position. He said, "I thank you for the offer, but I don't think I'll accept it."

"It's a good feeling. And it lets you, oh, get into yourself, sometimes in new ways."

"Is that good?"

Her face clouded. "It depends what you find. But if you find something bad, you tell yourself *I'm high, it's just the drug, and when I get straight again it won't apply.*"

"And that works?"

"For me."

"I was with several men once who used hashish. I mean that they used it in my presence, but I didn't partake. They didn't seem to be affected by it, and yet I gather they were very high."

"I had hash once."

"It's the same idea as marijuana, isn't it?"

"Well, like an orchestra is the same idea as a tin whistle. It's tons stronger. Where was this, that you were?"

"Morocco. No, Tunis."

"It must have been total dynamite. Tunis? What were you doing there?"

"Negotiating. There was an interest in mineral rights."

"You were with some corporation or something?"

"I represented them. Just in that series of negotiations. Nothing came of it."

She said, "I wonder about you, you know. For hours at a time.

12

About your life. Who are you. You paint all of these pictures, but I can never quite see you in any of the pictures."

"There's really nothing to see."

"Just a sweet quiet man who drinks mint tea."

"And watches robins."

"You know—"

"What?"

"Nothing," she said. She got to her feet. "I can't even pay you today and look, I stayed three hours, almost four. I guess I better go."

There was a brief moment when he could have asked her to stay for dinner. He recognized the moment and willed himself to let it pass.

"I'll be over Tuesday, then."

"Yes, good. And don't worry about the money. Please."

"I should have it by then."

"If you don't, it's no matter." He walked her toward the door. "I may be out of town," he said. "I can't be sure, and I don't know how long I would be away."

"The Turkish cigarette?"

"Yes. Something I might have to do."

He thought of the man who had smoked the Turkish cigarettes, and of the letter from Heidigger. Tampa. Jacksonville. Washington. His mind jumped through cities and time.

He said, "A favor."

"What?"

"One I've no right to ask. And can't honestly explain. Don't go to Washington tomorrow."

"I don't understand."

"Call it a feeling I have. I've learned to live on my intuition. I find it more reliable than pure reason. You've said your presence won't affect the demonstration any more than it in turn will affect policy. Indulge an old man. Spend the weekend here."

She looked at him. "All right," she said finally.

Twice more before the sky darkened he went to the kitchen window to watch the robins. The amount of work required of the parent birds was prodigious. They were constantly flying off and returning with worms to be thrust into gaping mouths.

He wondered why they bothered. Because they were robins, he thought, and that was what robins did.

Could they think, he wondered. Could they in any sense muse on the instinct, the irresistible urge to fill up the planet with copies of themselves? He decided they could not. The musers, the ponderers, would miss too many worms. They would build shaky nests. Cats would stalk them and pounce upon their reveries. And their seed would die, while less intellectual birds killed off the more thoughtful worms.

A wave of wholly unreal sadness enveloped him. "What shall I wish you?" he asked the birds, speaking aloud in English. "A long fruitful stupid life? Or fatal insight into the avian condition? Eh?"

He cooked some spaghetti. He used a bottled sauce, cooking a few sprigs of garden herbs into it. He drank a small glass of dry white wine with his supper.

Would she have enjoyed sharing this meal with him? Or would such an intimacy have made them nervous with each other?

A few minutes after nine he left his house and walked downtown. A neighbor, trimming a privet hedge with electric shears, waved to him as he passed. Dorn returned the greeting. At times he wondered what the neighbors thought of him. Probably they supposed he was doing something vaguely scholarly. A foreigner, a refugee, settled in a college town. No trouble, quiet, keeps to himself. Had they invented a role for Jocelyn? He smiled at the thought.

At nine-thirty he placed the call from a telephone booth in the hotel lobby. He told the operator his name was Leopold Vanders. A woman with a Latin accent answered on the third ring and accepted the call. The operator rang off. Dorn waited, saying nothing.

A man's voice said, "Mr. Vanders? I hope your decision is favorable."

"It is."

"Can we see you tomorrow? It would be three times better that way."

"Yes, I understand that."

"You received a letter today. The food is good there."

"All right."

"Until then."

The line went dead. He held the receiver for a moment, then replaced it. The voice was not one that he recognized. He was fair-to-good at American accents but would have had trouble placing this one with assurance. Kansas? Oklahoma?

14

He left the hotel. He walked the several blocks to his house and noted the spring in his step, the increased vitality. Did one ever retire?

The dining room of the Holiday Inn in Tampa at three in the afternoon. Until then.

TWO

Heidigger had a cowl

of longish white hair around the edges of his large bald head. He wore thick horn-rimmed glasses, a short-sleeved white shirt open at the throat, dark blue trousers, and blue crepe-soled canvas shoes. His face and arms were deeply tanned. His smile showed several gold teeth.

"Miles Dorn," he said. "Miles Dorn, Miles Dorn. Am I really to call you that?"

"It suits me."

"Miles Dorn. You know, I think it does. There is a thick, blunt honesty to it. Miles Dorn. Miles. Yes, it works. I believe you've lost weight, haven't you? I, on the other hand, have found some." He patted his belly. "But I am more at ease with it. I thought recently of those times in my life when I was thin. Never gaunt, mind you, but thin. Genuinely thin. I was also miserable, or in deep trouble. Often both. So I cannot regret my paunch. You did eat, I trust."

"Yes." He had taken a table downstairs and ordered a sandwich and iced tea. While he waited for it a young woman passed his table and repeated a three-digit number twice. After he had finished his sandwich he went to the room that matched that number. Heidigger, alone, admitted him.

"Do you like my room, Miles Dorn? In the past few years, I have discovered Holiday Inns. The most extraordinary institutions! There is at least one in any American city you could possibly have occasion to visit. The most unlikely places have them. And you know what is so remarkable about them? Not merely that they are clean and comfortable. One expects that in this country. The

15

big cars, you know. The soft seats in theaters. And the American bathroom. God, the American bathroom! I've heard it attributed to the Puritan heritage, a pathological absorption with cleanliness. Nonsense! Americans simply have an honesty that enables them to admit that human beings piss and shit and ought to be able to do so under the best possible circumstances. American toilet paper. I could write a monograph on American toilet paper. Have you ever stopped to think that this is quite possibly the only place in the world where a man can actually look forward to the prospect of wiping his asshole?"

"I hadn't, but I'm sure the thought will never be far from my mind. Eric, is this room clean?"

"Clean? Oh. Electronically? Yes, it's absolutely clean. Spotless. Unquestionably. Where was I? Yes! The institution of the Holiday Inn. It's my point that it is not the quality of these establishments that recommends them to me, or even the delicious impersonality of them, which in itself is such an absorbing commentary on the culture. Do you know what it is? It is their uniformity. Their uncanny uniformity. They are all the same. It doesn't matter where you go. St. Louis. Detroit. Tampa. San Francisco. Is there a Holiday Inn in Willow Falls, South Carolina?"

"I believe there is. Near the turnpike entrance. I have never been in it."

"You don't have to. Look around you. What you see here you would see there. No important differences. Take my word for it."

"Be assured that I do."

"Even the food is the same. Under no stretch of the imagination could it be called good. You could no more call it good than you could call it bad. It is Holiday Inn food, of a piece with everything else. But do you see how wonderful this is? Wherever I go, it is as if I have not traveled at all. My home is a room in a Holiday Inn, and as it is quite impossible to tell one of them from another, it is as if I am always at home in any city in the country. It has not yet happened, but some morning I will awaken and not know what city I am in. I will call the desk to ask them. 'I know this is the Holiday Inn, my dear. Be so good as to tell me which Holiday Inn. What city? What state?' It will happen."

Heidigger could not be hurried, nor did Dorn much want to

hurry him. One could hardly fail to respond to the man's effervescence. His unflagging good humor never deserted him. It was present at all times, while he stole, murdered, deceived, betrayed, subverted, and ruined. Dorn had often felt that it might be an important component in the man's habit of survival, which viewed rationally was difficult to explain. Their trade was capriciously hazardous in the best of circumstances. When one had Heidigger's genius for picking losing sides, one became singularly unattractive to insurance companies.

"Miles? You indulge me. You pay close and uncomplaining attention however far afield my conversation wanders. More than that, I cannot avoid flattering myself with the feeling that you actually enjoy listening to me."

"I actually do, Eric."

"Do you know something? I like you." He said this as if he found it remarkable. "I don't know if you are aware of this, but I once came very close to having you killed."

"In Prague."

"Prague? No. Oh, yes, then, but that was something else, that was not what I was thinking of. In Prague I would have killed you if the opportunity had come up, but it simply didn't. No, this was another time and another place, and I don't think I'll tell you where or when, but the suggestion was made to me that you ought to be terminated. A very strong suggestion from someone in a position to put forward suggestions strongly. Yet the matter was left to my discretion. I have never regretted the decision I made. I assure you I do not regret it now."

"Then I owe you my life, Eric. Eh?"

Heidigger stared for a moment, then laughed. He held his paunch in his hands and roared.

Heidigger said, "One wonders how much to tell someone. It varies with the person and with his role and with so many other situational factors. What elements need discussion? Money? With the least important men that is the most important topic to discuss. With you it is not. There is money here, Miles, Miles Dorn. We shall all feather our nests with this one. Which reminds me. Here. Take it. It is a token, an earnest, a guarantee of operating funds. It is only a thousand. Don't be shy, take it."

"I haven't said I'm in."

"But you are, aren't you? How easy is it for you to get out now? Don't look at me that way, that is not a threat; it is a practical statement. Consider. You want to know more before deciding. I want to say nothing to an uncommitted man. A stalemate? Not at all. You can change your mind and throw the money back. I can lie. Think. You have not been away from this so long, your head has not rusted. Think. Take the money. That's better.

"Now. Of course you must know about the area of operations. It is not Cuba. I understand that was a point of some concern to you."

"Yes."

"So." Heidigger threw himself into a chair, propped his elbows on its arms, made a steeple of his index fingers. "The country's name is immaterial. Not completely so, not ultimately, but in terms of giving you the situation, of highlighting it for you. So instead of naming our target area, I will tell you some things about it which I consider pertinent. Agreed?"

"Why not?"

"Good." A huge smile, gold teeth glittering. "We are concerned with a country which after a lengthy period of stability has been moving more and more into a state of revolutionary ferment. For decades almost all political opinion was religiously centrist. Now this is no longer the case. The left and right expand at the expense of the center.

"Leftist activity stems from two principal areas. As is almost invariably the case, the universities play a central role. There is a bookishness about the university radicals, but as their militancy increases this is less and less a factor. Further, there is a larger and larger circle of nonuniversity youth who look to the university radicals for political direction.

"Now. This country is biracial. The white population exists to a certain extent at the expense of the black population. The blacks have begun to depart from centuries of conditioning. They are becoming more vocal. As militancy becomes more and more a habit, the demagogues of the black left become increasingly extreme. Again a part of this process of polarization, if you will."

"That always happens," Dorn said. "I assume the black population constitutes a majority."

18

"No. Ten or fifteen percent. No more, although of course their birth rate is higher."

"Of course. Ten or fifteen percent. That surprises me."

"Higher in certain areas, of course."

"Yes. That does surprise me. I had been about to name the country and puncture your balloon. Instead it is I who am deflated."

Heidigger beamed. "No pins in my balloon, please. This is more than good theater, Miles. How easily your name fits into my speech! You've chosen well. More than good theater, though. There's method to it.

"To continue. The rightist reaction of the white *lumpenproletariat* is easily imagined. Their instinctive response is racist and anti-intellectual. They begin by living in terror of a black take-over. Simultaneously, and in much the same way, they dread the economic effects of a communist or quasi-communist revolution. Their preferred racial status permits them to see themselves as middle-class, and the bourgeoisie is invariably counterrevolutionary. Consider Cuba. The middle-class shopkeepers and professionals did not realize until they had helped the man to power that their own instincts are counterrevolutionary. Here, largely because of the racial situation, the reaction is more immediate. Here the militancy is just now emerging on a broad basis. Before the present, rightist activity was cultist. It was on the fringes. Now the lines are more clearly drawn. An effective demagogue has not yet surfaced on the right, but there are more and more confrontations with the university radicals, more and more groups forming with a broad base. There has been no consolidation of these groups, but that is only a question of time."

Dorn started to say something, but Heidigger showed his palm. "Another aspect is sectional. The southwestern fourth of the nation is its economic and political center. The rest of the country, the whites in the rest of the country, consider the southwesterners to be almost a separate tribe. A different nation. This is most strongly felt in the northwest, where the black concentration is greatest and where all of the obvious responses are intensified for the white lower class. It is also true throughout the East, and in rather a special way. There are entrenched economic interests in the East that feel almost completely alienated by that

19

core of southwestern money power. These people think of the southwest as Jew-influenced and pandering to the blacks at the expense of the rest of the country."

"What about the economy, Eric?"

"A long tradition of prosperity. Thirty years of noteworthy growth and stability. But a surprising incidence of poverty nevertheless. Black poverty, of course. White poverty in many areas, but most especially in the depressed northwest.

"Within the past two years, the economy has found its way into a state of chaos. Riotous inflation. Increasing unemployment, particularly black unemployment. Shares dropping off badly on the principal exchanges. This is a highly industrialized country, as you've perhaps gathered."

"Yes. It's also a Chinese puzzle. I can't think of what name to put to it." He touched his chin, the side of his nose. "I scarcely even read newspapers, you know. I've lost all touch with international politics."

"Then let me tease you some more. Certain things have occurred which would even make the pages of whatever sort of newspaper you have in Willow Falls, South Carolina. Did you ever think you'd come to live in a town with such a name, by the way? Certain events, I say, which if they ring no bell—this is a presentation, Miles, rather than a guessing game, though I can appreciate your temptation to play—certain events that may point up the directions the country is taking, the directions it might be coerced to take in the future.

"Politically, the national establishment is essentially oligarchic One of these ruling families—their orientation is left-centrist— has produced several charismatic political leaders, each of whom in a particular way managed to appeal to disparate portions of the local population. Two of them have been killed. Among the blacks, there have been considerably more liquidations, especially in the lower levels. But again there have been two very important murders recently, both of them removing dynamic and charismatic leaders who managed to mobilize their followers effectively without approaching the extreme positions of their rivals. You see the pattern, of course."

"From your words, it's unmistakable. These are the men who threaten the process of left-right polarization."

"Exactly so. Is that all? No. One final bit of information. The country has a long heritage of imperialism. It has a few remaining colonies and attempts to maintain a hold over them. This is to prove ultimately impossible, but in the meanwhile the country further depletes itself economically warring against guerrillas far from home."

"As the French did in Indo-China," Dorn said. "And learned not to do in Algeria."

"An excellent parallel. Now this military drain on national resources is universally deplored. The left opposes it as colonialist. The blacks oppose it for a variety of reasons. The right does and does not oppose it—they want it to end, they resent what it costs them, but their attitudes are largely formed in reaction to the attitudes of the left. Anything the left opposes they can scarcely help endorse. The military is like all armies everywhere, they would only give up this war if they could find a better one.

"Now. To come quickly to the point. I could give you more background but it would be purposeless. I want you first of all to put all guesses to the identity of the country from your mind."

"That's easily done. I'm at a standstill in that respect."

"And, taking as accurate my description of the situation, tell me what you think could happen."

Dorn got up, walked to the window. He looked down at traffic and tried to focus his mind on the country they had been discussing. He had some trouble doing this because he found it slightly less fascinating than the fact that Heidigger was giving him so much background information, was constructing such a theoretical case. He resisted the impulse to take this as ego food. Instead he was realistic enough to know that any employment of his services would be on a fairly low level. He was a tactician and not a strategist. He did not make policy. He was not to be consulted about policy. He was a common pirate, good with a cutlass, useful in tight places. But one did not ask him which ship to board. Why all of this theater? Heidigger was naturally theatrical but usually had a purpose for what he did. Where was the purpose hiding?

Reluctantly he turned from the window, dragging his mind back to the question. "All right," he said. "The answer I can give, the only answer I can give, is implicit in the question. In

21

your presentation. There are too many things left out. We have not discussed what the Russians will do, what the Americans will do, what the Chinese will do. We have not established in what sphere of influence the country lies. So I must rule out all these areas, and any relevant factor in these areas could completely determine where my answer should be. But that doesn't matter because this is a game or a presentation or whatever you choose to call it."

"You seem hostile."

"A little. I feel like a child reciting poems for family friends."

"I told you there was a method."

"All right. A scenario, then. The left will increase its provocations. They will be credited with some terrorism. If they do not think to perform it themselves, some equivalent of the Reichstag will go up in flames, with equivalent results. The left will not be able to focus its power. Its support base is far too small, and it will continue to be deprived of effective leadership, presumably through a continuation of the present policy of murder. The left will shrink and fragment itself even as it grows more extreme and militant. Am I reciting competently?"

"Oh, yes. You read with expression and carry yourself well."

"Thank you." It was silly, but he felt his hostility ebbing. "An effective demagogue will surface on the right. He will be well-financed—he had better be damn well-financed—by the dissident eastern financial interests, the ones who I gather have money and power but have had neither long enough to feel comfortable with them." He stopped for breath, bored with this performance, weary of his role in it. "When he emerges, the rightist fringe will abandon their little groups and quietly merge under his standard. His program will be anti-black and anti-Red and anti-intellectual. He will talk a great deal about the nation's destiny and rightful place in the world. He will blame the failure to liquidate the guerrillas on treason in high places. He will—the devil with him, I'm not going to write his fucking speeches, Eric."

"Go on."

"If it works, he will mobilize the *lumpenproletariat*—why does no other language have that word? It's essential. He will draw his strength from this group. His secondary strength will come from that large portion of the populace that is basically apolitical in more normal times. They will see him as a respite from chaos. The southwestern oligarchy will oppose him ineffectively and timidly until they discover they can no longer afford to oppose him. The more hardheaded ones will be killed. The Jews, if they've learned anything, which is perhaps doubtful, will come here or go to Israel. Oh."

"What?"

"Nothing." He spread his hands. "Shall I go on? He will appeal to the military. They may comprise much of his initial support. The southwestern money interests will think they can control him, just as his original financial supporters will think. If he's at all good, they will be wrong. He will repress the blacks, he will kill off the university radicals—I don't have to go on with this. The obvious parallel is Germany. The Weimar Republic. I wasn't around at the time, but what you've drawn is a word-picture of the Weimar Republic. If the man is Hitler, then he can be Hitler."

Heidigger was nodding encouragement. "Now the country," he said. "I know you have been feeling like a trained seal, Miles. You'll soon see why. Have you any ideas about the country?"

Dorn worried his lower lip. "Yes, I do," he said. "They came to me while I was talking. I think I know the country."

"Yes?"

"This is annoying. If I'm wrong, I will sound ridiculous. You see, I have not made any attempt to keep up with international politics. I have no idea what it's like over there politically or economically."

"I understand."

"I take it for granted that there are some purposeful inaccuracies in your story. That the blacks and the whites are not necessarily Negroes and Caucasians, for example. And that other elements have been rearranged in similar fashion."

"Go on. You fascinate me right now, Miles."

"Do I? The catch is that I am sure I would not care to operate there, and I am fucking certain you wouldn't. I don't think you could if you wanted to."

"Tell me the country. Now it's you who is being theatrical. Tell me the country."

Dorn said, "Israel. They've got their own country now, so

there's no sound reason why the Jews can't be fascists just like anyone else. The native Arabs are the blacks in your parable. The neighboring Arabs are the colonial guerrillas. I know nothing of their economy or politics, but the conditions you describe could conceivably exist there. And it explains another thing, damn it."

"What?"

"Your presentation. There has to be a payoff. All this can't lead up to some African shithole that I never heard the name of. It has to be outrageous; that's obviously why we're going through this intricate dance step. There are more outrageous things than Eric Heidigger engineering a fascist putsch in Israel, but I'd hate to have to list them."

"It's not Israel."

"No?" Dorn was surprised. "You didn't laugh."

"I was too staggered by the thought. Your mind does make nice jumps. King of the Jews! What a luscious notion. No, the situation is not right there at all, politically or economically. But it is an amazing thought, and I would not like to bet heavily that the conditions might not be right in five years or ten. Not that they're likely to invite us to come in."

"Do I have to guess again?"

"No." Heidigger bounced to his feet. "No! Enough guessing. I would be distraught if you guessed right. There was some trickery in my little speech. Not what you suspected—the blacks are black and the whites are white. Part of my deception was geographic. I turned the country upside down and backward. That is our objective, is it not? To turn the country upside down and backwards?"

"So the intellectual center—"

"Is not the southwest but the northeast. And the depressed area is not the northwest but the southeast. And the demagogue's financial backing comes not from the East but from the West." Heidigger's eyes flashed. Beads of sweat dotted his head. He was speaking louder and more intensely. "And the two charismatic left-centrists were brothers, and one of them was assassinated by an Arab and the other by a Cuban sympathizer. And the cops put down another of the niggers Wednesday.

"Do you see why I had to go through all that hypothetical drivel? Because otherwise you would have thought of a million reasons why it can't happen. The shit a man never sees is the

24

shit he's standing in. That's why the Jews didn't get out of Germany. They were too close to it. They were in the middle of it. They were up to their necks in shit before anyone even suggested opening a window.

"But you took the facts and wrote the script, Miles Dorn. You can't say it can't be done. You just said *how* it can be done." He threw himself down in the chair again. He folded his arms, put his left foot on his right knee. "It can be done," he said, his voice at whisper level now. "Everything's right. Everything. It will fall in our laps."

Dorn was white. He was shivering, and could barely keep his balance. The floor seemed miles away. Miles from Croatia. Vertigo. That was her cat's name, Vertigo.

"In our laps," he heard Heidigger saying. His voice seemed far off, faint, filtered. "The United States of America. In our laps."

THREE

It had been perhaps

twenty years since Dorn read *Der Fragebogen*, but whole passages of it were etched on his mind. The book was an autobiography couched in the form of an acerbically whimsical response to a questionnaire prepared at the war's close for an Allied denazification program. The author was Ernst Von Salomon, Walther Rathenau's assassin and a highly placed writer and editor Goebbels' propaganda ministry.

Dorn, a Croat, had spent the war years with Ante Pavelic, killing Serbs and Titoist partisans. He had not been subject to any equivalent of denazification. It had simply been necessary for him to leave Yugoslavia. Yet there had been much in Von Salomon's arrogant apologia that struck chords then that echoed twenty years later.

Now, hunched on an aisle seat of a speeding Greyhound bus, he particularly recalled one passage. Von Salomon, a fascist activist since the twenties, discussed the dismay with which he

25

and several close friends regarded the Hitler regime during its first years. These were young men, Von Salomon and his friends. Idealists. Patriots. Visionaries. They despised the Austrian corporal and his Brownshirts. How then to explain their subsequent acts?

"Together we swore an oath. There were two things we would not do. We would not commit suicide, and we would not leave the country."

Dorn had never made the mistake of crediting *Der Fragebogen* with any particular relationship to truth. One did not, after all, cultivate a reverence for truth in the ministry of propaganda, nor did one learn credulity in Dorn's life schools. But that three-sentence explanation, awful in its simplicity, had an irresistible ring to it. From a simple negative decision against death and emigration all the rest of it flowed like water.

Dorn could scarcely remember being a young man. He had never been an idealist, a patriot, a visionary. Thoughts of both death and departure were oddly comforting.

But survival was a habit he had acquired, and flight a habit he had given up. He was not given to oaths, but he, like Von Salomon, recognized two things he would not do. He would not commit suicide, and he would not leave the country.

A ten-minute rest stop somewhere in Georgia. Dorn used the lavatory, shut himself in a stall. The toilet bowl was stained, the seat's plastic cover cracked, the floor filthy. The toilet paper dispenser provided little squares of airmail stationery one at a time. The American bathroom, indeed!

(Before he left Heidigger, during a conversational lapse, Dorn had suddenly said, "But they have no bidets." And to Heidigger's blank look he had explained, "The American bathrooms that you praised. They have no bidets. Perhaps that could be embodied in our leader's program."

Heidigger had bounced up. "But there *is* a bidet! In my very bathroom. In this Holiday Inn." Dorn said he hadn't noticed it.

"Go in now. See for yourself."

"I'll take your word for it."

"But there is no need to take my word for it. Take ten steps and see for yourself. If you were a young lady, I would invite

26

you to have a complimentary douche, but at least you may see for yourself."

He had laughed sharply, laughter that Heidigger had not understood. "Eric," he had said at length, "Eric, I am not going to examine your bidet. I am going to trust you that there is a bidet in your bathroom. Eric, if I cannot trust you on the matter of a bidet in a bathroom, then we are in serious trouble.")

He sat on the toilet and read capsule biographies, written on plain typing paper in a feminine hand. Written with a fountain pen—Leopold Vanders also used a fountain pen, albeit a different one. Was that to be a trademark of the movement? He hadn't seen a fountain pen in years, wasn't aware that they still manufactured them.

John Lowell Drury.

Senior senator from New Hampshire. Kennedy loyalties and political philosophy. Democratic presidential aspirant. Late but strong antiwar stand. Early antipollution stand. Economic left-centrist. Strongest support from non-radical students. Insignificant black support. Good image with white middle class. Record acceptable to organized labor. Effective speaker, frequent university appearances. Speedy termination advised, preferably via identifiable leftist. This cover may be transparent. Age: 49. Married. One child. Residence: (Washington): 2115 Albemarle; (Berlin, New Hampshire): 114 Carrollton Place . . .

Emil Karnofsky.

Director, National Brotherhood of Clothing Workers. Member, national board, AFL-CIO. Jew. First major labor leader to take antiwar position. Union membership chiefly black, Puerto Rican. Respected by colleagues but regarded as New York Jew leftist. Termination advised to foster solidarity in labor circles. Strongly recommend termination via natural causes or accident. If unavoidably otherwise, political motivation must not be suggested. Age: 77. Widower. Three children, eight grandchildren . . .

27

William Roy Guthrie.

Three-term governor of Louisiana. Presidential candidate, Free American Party, 1964, 1968. Sectionalist demagogue with minor racist appeal in industrial Midwest. Controlled alcoholic. Insufficient stature and character for national leadership. Political program neopopulist, negative. Termination advised to allow his personal following in the southeast to flow into the movement. Termination of Guthrie must precede termination of Theodore. Thrust may come from black extremist or university radical. This cover should be opaque. Age: 57. Married. No children . . .

Walter Isaac James.

First-term mayor of Detroit. Black. Economic and social moderate. Foreign policy views unstated. Enjoys near-total support of black constituency plus strong support of white power structure, professionals, intellectuals. Relationship improving with white working class. Efficient administrator. Termination acceptable via black extremists or white racists, though latter slightly preferable. Termination ideally to be as dramatic as possible. Perhaps family could be included. Age: 44. Married. Five children . . .

Patrick John O'Dowd.

Second-term mayor of Philadelphia. Liberal Republican. National aspirations. Charismatic. Social radical, economic conservative. National appeal to youthful left-centrists. Strong secondary black appeal. Focal point of white working-class hatred throughout eastern seaboard. Termination recommended but not urgent. Natural or accidental termination advised. Age: 47. Married . . .

Henry Michael Theodore.

Vice-President, United States of America. An intuitive political amateur with an instinctive appreciation of centrist and right-centrist anxieties. A refined demagogue. Romanian ancestry, original name Teodorescu. Theodore's moderate right-centrist stance and his extraordinary success at focusing white middle-class discontent make his termination a quintessential ingredient in movement policy. It should be scheduled at least one and no more than three months after Guthrie's termination. Terminal thrust must be unmistakably via large-scale leftist conspiracy. Involvement should extend to both black and white radicals. N.B.—It is imperative that the terminal cover be wholly opaque. Not only must there be no official or unofficial suspicion of movement involvement, but there can be no evidence of any involvement that is not absolutely identifiable as leftist and/or black. Age: 62. Married. One child, one grandchild . . .

He paused on his way out of the men's room to wash his hands with liquid soap. As he dried them in a stream of hot air, a wall scribble caught his eye.

"*If you are not part of the solution,*" he read, "*then you must be part of the problem.*"

Heidigger had said, "If you could take them in order, so much the better. But it's not vital. Only that Guthrie goes before Theodore."

"I imagine there are other lists."

"Not on this level of priority. There will be a great many incidents which we will help to develop. Riots, confrontations. But I should be surprised if half of what occurs during the next six months is our work. All of this"—a hand flung out to indicate the world—"would eventually come to pass without us. We lend it direction."

"You expect these six in six months?"

"Just the first four. O'Dowd is less important than the others. If you can't get to him in hot weather, you might almost as well skip him entirely."

"I thought he was supposed to go quietly."

"So they say. I think he should go out loud, that he's only worth taking out if it makes the niggers burn down Philadelphia. Hot weather for Walter Isaac James, of course. Anyway, figure six months' lead time. And then the date for Theodore is mid-October. You come as close to that as you can, but no later than the last week of the month."

29

"The election is next year."

"What a quick mind! But some states hold off-year gubernatorial elections."

"Oh."

"And the bigger our man wins, the better he looks next year."

"I gather I don't get to learn his name."

"Not today. But don't shoot any governors except for Guthrie. Just to be on the safe side."

"I don't know if I can do all these."

"It's what you do, Miles, and you do it as well as anyone I have ever known."

"I have been known to miss."

"Not often."

"And these are not six nonentities. There's not only security in front but the certainty of a stench afterward. The Vice-President, for Christ's sake."

"No one's safe if you want him. No one on earth. Who knows this better than you?"

He acknowledged this with silence, then looked thoughtfully at Heidigger. His voice softened. "Why should I do this, Eric? You expect me to do it. You and I both sit here expecting that I will do it. Why is this so?"

"You'll act for the good of the country. To preserve the American Way of Life. Bathrooms and Holiday Inns."

"The question was serious."

"So was the answer. Do you know what happens if we don't act? Do you know? Chaos. Literally, chaos. The trends continue. Polarization increases. The left retains certain strengths. The right is too splintered to take control. The economy goes completely to hell. The center evaporates like piss on a hot iron. The cities erupt. Pointless bloodbaths. Utter disorder. That is the alternative, Miles Dorn. The mistake everyone makes is to believe that the alternative to change is preservation of the status quo. And this is so rarely true. The alternative to change is another sort of change. You know this."

"No, I don't know it. Perhaps it is true—"

"It is."

"—But I do not know it. I have no politics, Eric. You know that. I do not act out of principles."

"Who does, in our line?"

"You do. You have standards, you have a set political frame of reference. I do not."

"Then perhaps that is why you can do this sort of thing so much better than I. I can point. You can act. Perhaps that is why."

"But why do I do it? Why, Eric?"

"Because it is how you are defined, how you define yourself. You do it because it is what you do."

"Like robins."

"I don't hear you."

"Nothing," he said. "A private thought."

"Enjoy your private thoughts. It's a free country."

Back on the bus, head flung back, half in and half out of sleep, he played with private thoughts while the bus coursed northward through a free country.

A governor, a senator, a labor leader, two mayors. A vice-president. Worms to feed my baby robins. Men to nourish worms.

If you are not part of the solution, then you must be part of the problem.

FOUR

Monday noon she rang his bell. He was not surprised to see her. He had been expecting her ever since he read the morning paper.

"Oh, God," she said.

She was ashen-faced, trembling. He took her arm.

"You know about it."

"I read about it, yes."

"I wasn't supposed to come until tomorrow. If you're busy—"

"I have a completely free afternoon. Come in."

"I have the five dollars."

31

"You're being hysterical. Come inside. Now sit down. Would you like anything? Tea? A glass of wine?"

"No," she said. She took hold of her upper arms, hugged herself, shuddered. She sighed heavily. Then she said, "I'm all right now."

"Are you sure you wouldn't like some wine?"

"No." Her eyes found his face. In German she said, "Your intuition saved my life."

"Oh, now."

"Fourteen of them. Dead. Fourteen kids dead. It was never fourteen before. But when it was four at Kent State, everybody said, 'God, it was never four before.'" She had returned to English. "And thirty-five wounded. One of them was from here. You know that, you saw the paper. What you don't know was that he was a friend of mine. They didn't put that in the paper. 'Jon Yerkes, 20, who was shot through the wrist and is expected to lose the use of his right hand, was a friend of Jocelyn Perry.' *Is* a friend. He's still alive. He just doesn't have a right hand any more. He played the guitar. *Played*. Not *plays*. You need two hands to play a guitar. God, I can't relate to that. I was up all night. We were all up all night. Kids went around smashing windows because they couldn't think of anything else to do. Nonviolent kids went around the campus smashing windows. I can't relate to any of this. Look, Ma, no hand. Oh."

She got to her feet. "I said I was all right. I'm not. I think I have to throw up."

Was it one of Heidigger's? Or did it just happen?

A confrontation. Students and National Guard. Some students broke the demonstration's nonviolent code, shouted insults, hurled rocks. (Student radicals? Or plants?) A couple of guardsmen used their rifle butts on demonstrators. (Because it was necessary? Because they couldn't take the pressure? Or because they were following private orders?) More students responded with rocks. A shot was or was not fired from the crowd. (Was there a shot? Was it a student who fired it?) A guardsman fired a shot in return, killing a student. Then there was definitely gunfire from the crowd, from several points in the crowd, and the guard returned fire. Fourteen students dead, dead. Thirty-five wounded. Look, Ma.

It could have happened by itself, Dorn knew. As it had happened before, as it would happen again. Spontaneously, a flash flood, a fire in a hayloft.

Or it could have been handled by three men after a scant hour's planning.

Which?

He didn't know that it mattered.

"I might have been standing next to Jon Yerkes. We would have been together. I could have been between him and that bullet."

"You could have stayed here and walked in front of a bus. Don't torture yourself with hypotheses."

"I can think you saved my life if I want to."

("Then I owe you my life, Eric. Eh?")

"I found the different reactions of public officials interesting," Dorn said. She was calmer now. They had chatted in German about assorted trivia. She had looked at the baby robins—it was surprising how quickly they grew—and accepted a cup of mint tea. "It interests me how everyone prominent has something to say, and how they can all find such different lessons in the same incident."

"Like the President," she said bitterly. "Our great leader. 'We must all work together to repair this tragedy. There must be mutual disarmament. Students must not throw rocks, and the Brownshirts must use smaller-caliber rifles.'"

"And the Vice-President."

"Sweet old Theodorable. According to him, this proves that protest is self-defeating. In other words, if somebody's jumping up and down on your back, you'd better lie there quietly so you don't get him really mad. Oh, God, I hate that man. When I see him on television I want to kick the screen in. Somebody ought to put a bullet through that head of his."

He started. "Do you mean that? Or is that rhetoric?"

"I don't even know." Frowning, "I'm nonviolent. I mean I've always been nonviolent. I don't like window-breaking or any of that. I mean, how can you protest violence by hurting people? But I keep feeling myself going through changes. It's weird, like

33

I'm being led through things. That man is tearing the country apart, and the more he does it the more the idiots applaud. I think he's a dangerous man. I think—I don't know."

"And yet the Vice-President sounded moderate enough compared to Governor Guthrie."

"That rotten fascist bastard."

"Did you hear what he was quoted as saying?"

"I don't think I want to hear. I can imagine. Oh, tell me."

"I won't get the words right, but the essence was that if any Red anarchist hippie niggerlovers tried that sort of thing in Louisiana, it would be the last time any of those hands had the life to pick up rocks."

"He actually said that." It wasn't a question. "The son of a bitch."

"And he added something about machine guns."

"Oh, I hope somebody gets him," she said. "I'm not *that* nonviolent. I think it would be worth dying, to get someone like Guthrie first."

"Of course, there were other voices, too. Several senators called for an investigation of the guard's role. And there was one senator, I think from New Hampshire or Vermont, I can't remember his name."

"You mean Drury? The White Hope?"

"Is that what they call him?"

"I don't know. Some people do."

"I thought he put things very well. He said that dissent could not be repressed, but then he took it a step further. He said neither could dissent be ignored. That dissenting elements in our society had to be accommodated not only for their sake but for the sake of society itself. What's the matter? You look enormously unimpressed."

"I don't know. Oh, shit, what good does it do? He's been saying that for years. Each time something happens he says it and each time it's true and each time everybody claps and each time nothing happens, and now J. Lowell Drury is up there again saying get out of Vietnam and stop the pollution and stop killing the Panthers and the students, and the only difference is that last time Jon Yerkes had two hands and this time he has one."

"I wonder, then. Doesn't a man like Drury do any good at all?"

"I don't know if he does or not." She nibbled at a fingernail. "What a lot of people say, what they've been saying all along, is that someone like that does more harm than good. Because he's on your side, you know, he really is, it's not bullshit, he means it. And he's part of the system. And what he says and does makes people think maybe there's hope working through the system."

"And there isn't?"

"Well, is there? The Democrats wouldn't nominate Drury, and if they did, he wouldn't win, but suppose he did. So he takes office, J. Lowell Drury of New Hampshire, and the first day the generals take him aside and whisper in his ear, and the next day the businessmen take him aside and whisper in his ear, and if he's lucky the CIA takes him aside and whispers in his ear, and like he's part of the Establishment and he can't turn his ear off when these people whisper in it, and so the third night he goes to bed in the White House and when he wakes up in the morning he's not J. Lowell Drury anymore, he's Hubert Humphrey."

And, a few moments later. "I don't know. I like Drury. I see him on television and I like him."

"But you wonder if the country would be any worse off than it already is without him."

"Right." Eyes wide, empty. "And I can't see how it would."

"It really helped to talk to you, Miles. You're the only older person I know that I can rap with. And I can get a better set on things from talking with you. The other kids. We always say the same things to each other."

"It does me good to talk to you."

"How could it?"

"In precisely the same way. And because I would find your company enjoyable in and of itself if we talked of nothing more profound than baby birds."

"Baby birds can be profound."

"I know."

"There was a book in our high school library called *A Mouse Is Miracle Enough*. I never read it, but I flashed on the title." In German she repeated the title. And in English again, "I like just talking with you, too. In any language, and about anything."

"Forget about the lessons," he said. "I've felt uncomfortable taking money from you for weeks now. And my schedule is going to be chaotic for the next few months. Come over whenever you feel like it. If I'm home, we'll talk. In German, in English."

She looked intently at him. He wondered if he had said more than he should have. The next instant her face melted into a rich warm liquid smile.

"You were my teacher," she said, "and now you are my friend."

"Miles? I was just thinking. You really got into what happened in Washington in a heavy way. I was surprised."

"Oh?"

"I always had this impression of you that you really weren't a political person."

"I'm not. I was politically concerned in Europe for many years. When I was able to settle comfortably in America, I thought one could remain uninvolved."

"But today—"

"Perhaps it was that a victim was a boy from the college here. Yerkes. When I saw that in the paper—"

"I can imagine."

"I felt an involvement for the first time. Or perhaps I should say a concern."

"Right," she said. "That's it. When it reaches out and touches someone close to you, that's what brings it all home, isn't it?"

"Yes."

FIVE

Dorn flew to Boston and rode buses North. On the Caldwell campus in Maine, a student told him that the newspaper office was in the Student Union, and another student told him where the Union was. In the office of the Caldwell *Clarion* there were two girls at large black typewriters and a long-haired boy reading *Cat's Cradle*. One of the girls asked Dorn if she could help him.

"I called before," he said. "Somebody said if I came down,

I could pick up copies of the last half-dozen issues or so. See, I have this pizza stand on the highway and I was thinking about maybe running an ad."

"Our advertising manager isn't here now—"

"Well, I would just want to look at the papers and then I would get in touch later."

"I can certainly help you there," she said. There were rows of newspapers stacked on a long table. She walked the length of the table, taking a paper from each stack. She said, "Will this be enough? And I'm giving you a rate card, too. The rates are printed in each issue, but the information on the card is more complete, the cost of running cuts and everything."

"This'll do it, then."

"And if you'll give me your name, I'll have Dick get in touch with you as soon as he comes around."

"Oh, never mind about that. It's easier for me if I get in touch, with my hours and all."

"I'm sure an ad in the *Clarion* would be profitable for you."

"Yeah, well, that's what I was thinking. Pull in business and all."

"I would certainly think so. What was the name of your pizza place? I don't think I got it."

"You know the one. Right out on the highway."

"Oh," she said. "That one. Uh-huh."

From the hallway he heard the boy say, "Now why in the hell would you do an immoral thing like hustle that poor guy for an ad? I don't get it."

"He wanted to advertise."

" 'I'm sure an ad would be profitable for you.' What utter bullshit! 'Let's go out for a slice of pizza, I saw this outasight ad in the *Clarion*.' Jesus Christ."

"Somebody has to pay for the fucking paper."

"Yeah. *What* pizza place on the highway?"

"You know the one. Come on, Paul. Who *cares* what pizza place on the highway? Who cares what highway?"

From an issue of the Caldwell *Clarion*:

"Administration sources disclosed today that Caldwell commencement exercises would be moved up to the second weekend in May to facilitate the appearance of Sen. J. Lowell Drury of

New Hampshire. Arrangements have already been made for Senator Drury to deliver the commencement address. Much in demand on the graduation circuit, the New Hampshire liberal . . ."

From another issue of the Caldwell *Clarion*:

"Burton Weldon, former chairman of the now-disbanded Caldwell chapter of Students for a Democratic Society (SDS) yesterday attacked the selection of Sen. J. Lowell Drury as commencement speaker. 'Drury has no relevance whatsoever to the current situation. He wants us to love him because he's a liberal,' Weldon told the *Clarion*. 'I see no reason why anyone whose head is together would waste time sitting through his speech. All he'll do is put a sugar coating on the same old Establishment pill. It's a special kind of pill. You take it when you're feeling good, and it makes you sick.' Pressed for his ideal choice for commencement speaker, Weldon said, 'There's nobody. Everybody worth hearing is in jail.' Asked about rumored plans to disrupt the exercises, Weldon sharply shot down the rumor. 'The world is past that stage,' he avowed. 'What good are signs and slogans when the Establishment is using guns?' "

From a third issue of the Caldwell *Clarion*:

"Campus radical Burton Weldon refused to confirm or deny imputations that his comments criticizing Sen. J. Lowell Drury constituted the implicit endorsement of violence. 'I stand by my words,' the former chairman of the now-disbanded Students for a Democratic Society (SDS) announced. 'People can read into them whatever they want. After all, they're just words. They aren't bullets.' Speaking in sharp rebuttal, Harry Isenberg of the Caldwell Liberal Alliance for Peace (CLAFP) termed his phrases 'irresponsible, inflammatory, and . . .' "

Dorn leaned over the counter, weighing the new reel in his hand. "Can you believe it?" he said. "I drove all the way to Vermont. I was actually at the stream before I discovered that my reel was rusted solid. Now I can't believe I put it away wet, but I guess I did."

"Sometimes they'll loosen up for you," the man behind the counter said. "More trouble than it's worth, most likely. And they'll never be the same as they were. How are you for bait? Hooks?"

"Strictly a fly-fisherman, and I'm in good shape on everything else. On everything, now that I've got the reel. Say, I was noticing those guns when I came in. What do you have to go through to purchase a rifle in Vermont?"

"Have to be a resident."

"I thought as much. And then you probably have to have a firearms card with your fingerprints on it."

"Nope, just a resident driver's license. Where you from?"

"Pennsylvania."

"And you've got a lot of red tape down there, do you?"

"They've made it just about impossible to buy a gun."

"Ayeh. I'd say that's what they have in mind, wouldn't you say?" He leaned his weight on the counter. "It's different up here. I'll tell you. You people have a situation with the colored. There are all those colored, so naturally a white man wants to arm himself. Way the government must see it, the more people with guns the more shooting is going to happen." He winked, a gesture that astonished Dorn. "Put it this way, at least they can't sell them to the colored either. Be thankful for small things, eh?"

The boy made himself comfortable on the car seat and asked if it was okay to smoke. Dorn told him to go ahead. The boy lit a cigarette and rolled down the window to flip the match out, then rolled the window up again.

"Nice car," he said.

"It belongs to a friend. I borrowed it."

"That's the kind of friend to have."

The boy was about 20, 5′ 9″, 140 pounds. Burton Weldon, former chairman of the now-disbanded Caldwell chapter of Students for a Democratic Society, was 21, 5′ 10″, 150 pounds. This boy was clean-shaven and had short hair. Weldon's hair was long and he wore a Zapata moustache.

"You live here in Vermont?"

"Yes, sir. In Hazelton."

"Can you drive? That's the main reason I stopped, to be frank. My head is splitting and I don't want to take chances with a friend's automobile. You can drive?"

"Since I was fifteen."

"You have a license? You have it with you, I mean."

"Always carry it."

"You wouldn't mind driving?"

"A car like this? You kidding?"

Dorn pulled to a stop. He turned to face the boy. "Tell me," he said. "What do you think of J. Lowell Drury?"

"Who's he?"

"You don't recognize the name?"

"I don't think so. Is that your name or something?"

"Interesting you never heard of him," Dorn said. "You helped to murder him."

"Huh?"

"Your role was a small one. A spear carrier. You stole this automobile. Then you lost control of it and crashed it into one of those trees, I think. You weren't wearing your seat belt."

"Mister, I don't think—"

"You died in the accident," Dorn said, reaching, hands quick and accomplished. He cupped the back of the short-haired head with his right hand, caught up the shirtfront with his left. He snapped the boy's neck forward. There was no struggling. There was no time.

The boy's license was in his wallet. The boy had automatically tapped a pocket when Dorn asked him about the license. That was the pocket he looked in, and the wallet was there. He took the license, replaced the wallet. The boy's name was—had been? no, was—Clyde Farrar, Jr.

He propped Clyde Farrar, Jr., behind the wheel, left his seat belt unfastened. Dorn sat on the passenger side. He started the engine and steered with one hand. His own seat belt was fastened, and he was braced when the car hit the tree.

Before he entered a second sporting goods store, this one considerably closer to the Maine border, he used a pencil to change Farrar's date of birth from 1950 to 1920. His signature on the bill of sale for the deer rifle would have fooled anyone but a handwriting expert. The clerk didn't look at it twice, or at the altered date of birth, for that matter.

He changed it back after he left the store.

A long-distance telephone conversation:
"Hello. You received the funds?"
"Yes. Something else occurs to me."
"Oh?"

40

"It would be best if there were no academic difficulty in my home district."

"We never considered it. That's an undeveloped district, after all."

"Like so many, it has some surface tension. Admittedly of low density. I wouldn't want the waters troubled. It would spoil my own swimming."

A chuckle. "As it happens, you have exclusive representation in your district. Now that you mention it, it might be worthwhile to assign someone in a conciliatory capacity."

"Try it again."

"You're swimming alone, but if the water's troubled we can send you some oil."

"Understood, but no. It's my backwater."

"Delicious. Anything else?"

"No."

Another long-distance telephone conversation:

"Hello? Hey, turn that down, huh? Hello?"

"Is that you, Roger?"

"Yeah. Who's this?"

"Burt."

"I can't hear you, man."

"Burt Weldon."

"Man, this is a shit connection. You got to talk louder, you sound like you're coming through a roomful of Dacron or something. Is it Burt?"

"Right on, baby. Burt Weldon."

"Like I can just barely make you out. What's happening?"

"Everything's happening, man. Everything."

"You cool, man? You sound kind of weird."

"I'm beautiful. I want you to recognize it when it happens."

"Huh?"

"I want you to know where it came from."

"You sure you're all right? It's Burt Weldon, baby, I don't know what he wants. He sounds really weird, totally fucked up. He never used to use anything. Hey, Burt? What kind of trip are you on?"

"The ultimate trip."

"Whatever's cool."

41

"The ultimate cool. A trip down Drury Lane. That's all I can say."

"Whatever it is I couldn't hear it."

"I said a trip down Dreary Lane. We all know the Muffin Man."

"Huh?"

Dorn set up the portable typewriter in his motel room. On a sheet of plain typing paper he typed:

> To the good people, who are dead or in jail:
>
> No one will understand this. Maybe that proves it was the right thing to do. The things the world understands always turn out wrong.
>
> Does the end justify the means? I no longer comprehend the question. Once I knew the question but did not know the answer. Now I know the answer but have lost my grasp of the question.
>
> We tried words. Words are out-of-date. Dreary Drury gives us words, and we throw back bullets.
>
> It seems to me

An hour later he went to the off-campus apartment house where Burton Weldon lived. He traded the typewriter for Weldon's, which was open on the desk. He put a box of shells for the deer rifle on the closet shelf and covered it with a dirty shirt. He crumpled the unfinished letter and dropped it in a corner of the room where several crumpled sheets of paper already nestled.

He left with Weldon's typewriter in hand.

The night before commencement exercises he had a dream in Serbo-Croat.

For some time now English had been his language of thought as well as his language of speech. Certain idioms might occur, in thought as in speech, in any of several languages; there were certain concepts that did not translate. But it was English that he both thought and spoke.

Dreams might come in any language. Lately they had been

most often in English, but as recently as a year ago they had been primarily in German. He also dreamed occasionally in Serbo-Croat, and now and again in French.

There was usually a connection between the language of the dream and its subject matter. Dreams of his youth, for example, were most likely to be in Serbo-Croat. Dreams of the present were often in English. But there was no hard and fast rule. Dreams, possessing their own system of logic, had their own scheme of comparative linguistics as well.

This dream, set in the present time, was nevertheless in Serbo-Croat.

In the dream he was in the chemistry laboratory. Its window high in the Science Building overlooked the quadrangle where commencement exercises were to be held. And he talked in the dream to Burton Weldon, who was dead in the dream, already shot down by guardsmen in retribution for a crime Miles Dorn had not yet got around to perpetrating. Though dead, Burton Weldon was able to hear and to speak; miraculously, he was able to understand and to speak Serbo-Croat.

Furthermore, Weldon's face wouldn't behave. It kept turning into the face of Clyde Farrar, Jr.

When the time came to shoot Drury, his dream finger froze on the dream trigger. He pulled with all his strength but was not strong enough to make his finger move.

The speech went on and on and on, with Sen. J. Lowell Drury (Dem., N.H.) orating in flawless Serbo-Croat. And then the speech ended, and Drury left the podium, and still the finger had not moved the trigger.

"You see?" Burton Weldon's corpse shrilled at him. "You see? You could not do it!"

He awoke drenched in sweat, fighting his way out of the dream, fighting Weldon's voice (but it was not Weldon's voice in the dream; it was someone else's; whose?) and clawing at the bed-clothing with hands and feet. He went into the bathroom and stood for a long time under the shower, thinking about the dream.

He knew enough of dream theory to recognize it as a classic impotence syndrome. Virility anxiety. The gun is a penis, and one cannot make it work. And yet it was so specific, and so much related to present circumstances, that he was not certain whether it was in fact a sexual dream or more an indication of unconscious fear that he would fail to kill Drury.

Was it the same thing? Was the gun a penis in his life as well as in his dreams? He had thought of this before, of course. He was too insightful not have had the thought, too honest to dismiss it peremptorily, and yet too hardened to dwell on it.

Later, after he had made the last of the arrangements, set up a meeting with Weldon, scattered more bits of damning evidence (but not too many, and never too obviously; let them work, those cops; they loved to find elusive clues)—after everything was set and checked out, he realized whose dream voice had spoken Serbo-Croat words through Burton Weldon's dead lips.

Jocelyn's.

This, more than anything else about the dream, gnawed at him.

SIX

Jocelyn sat, legs crossed, a hand at her chin. "You know," she said, "when I heard about it I thought of you right away. Some of the things we were talking about before you left. And I wasn't surprised when it happened, that's another thing. That's the thing, nobody was surprised. Somebody was listening to a radio and came down the hall passing the word, and hardly anybody was surprised. As if we all knew they would get him sooner or later. They get everybody."

"But the boy was a leftist, wasn't he?"

"If he did it."

"I didn't follow the reports too closely," Dorn admitted. "But I understood it was open-and-shut."

"It always is, isn't it? Who always gets shot? Kennedy. King. Bobby. Malcolm. Drury. They're always leftists, and they always get shot by leftists."

"Not King."

"No, but it might have looked that way if they hadn't caught that guy. And even so they want you to believe that there wasn't a conspiracy, that this Ray broke out of prison and did it all by himself. Nobody believes that. Nobody believes the Warren Commission. I don't think I've ever met anybody who believes the Warren Commission. And when Bobby Kennedy was killed, well, they caught him right there, he did it, but somebody must have put the idea in his head. I mean, he was this mixed-up little Arab; somebody must have put the idea in his head."

"I see what you mean. And Weldon?"

"I guess he flipped out. The letter he started to write, and he evidently made some strange telephone calls. And he was supposed to be in an accident in a stolen car, and then he used a dead boy's driver's license to buy a gun in Vermont. Or else he had someone buy it for him. But other people said he was on campus in Caldwell when the accident took place."

"Perhaps he had an accomplice."

"Maybe." She looked doubtful. "I guess he was very militant. So many kids, though. They talk more than they act. That's part of the game, putting the Establishment uptight. Of course if he flipped out, and then they say he called somebody and said he realized Drury was his father. You know, if he was in that whole Oedipus bag—"

Was there anyone so easily manipulated as the amateur at revolution? They were suspicious, cautious, their caution occasionally verging on paranoia. They accepted it as highly likely that any adult was a policeman. But they did not honestly believe that anything could happen to them. They were young, and that damned them because the young always assume themselves to be immortal and immune. They may state flatly that they expect to die, that they do not expect the planet itself to survive another ten years. But the idea of personal death, of sudden pointless personal death, is never real to them.

And so they are oddly careless. It was easy to arrange a secret meeting with Burton Weldon, easy to mention a few of the correct names and phrases, easy to win not his trust but his physical presence.

"You may be a cop, man. Let's say that I take it for granted you're a cop."

But, taking it for granted, he still told no one where he was going or whom he was meeting, he still met with Dorn and went into the Science Building with him, mounted the flights of stairs, entered the chemistry lab.

"The funeral was on television yesterday," she said. "A lot of kids watched it. Even some of the ones who had gone around saying that Drury was just a knee-jerk liberal. They changed their attitudes completely the minute his body was cold. I didn't watch the funeral."

"A show," Dorn said. "Entertainment for the public."

"That's all it is. And I was thinking. There was no big tele-vised funeral for the fourteen kids who died in Washington. Someone was saying that they ought to put Burt Weldon's funeral on television. You know, under the equal-time code."

"There's a bitter thought."

"If Weldon even did it. But I guess there's no doubt, is there? I mean, he was right there with the gun in his hands."

"I was told to contact you," he said, "because of your feelings toward Drury."

"My feelings? The whole point of it is that I haven't got any feelings about him. He doesn't exist. He's not relevant."

"Some people feel he ties marginal revolutionaries to the Establishment."

"No question. So?"

"So perhaps we might return bullets for his words, as you suggested."

"Hey, don't turn it around on me, man. I don't know you. I don't know what you want to make my words do."

"I'll be honest with you, Weldon. I was sent here to give Mr. Drury a bullet."

"Oh, wow!"

"I need assistance."

"From me?"

"Yes."

"You're going to shoot him from here. From the window. Wow. Listen, I don't really know that this is my kind of thing. I don't know that I'm ready for it, if you follow me."

"You can see the political value."

46

"*Radicalize* more people. Create confrontation. Cut out the phony liberal alternative. It's obvious. I'm not an idiot."

"And you approve?"

"I don't know. I guess so."

"And you'll help?"

"How?"

"Have a car ready for me in back. I would do my own driving, but you could get the car in position for me. Then, when the time comes, you could create a diversion. A minor disruption, some egg throwing, perhaps. Something to confuse them for a moment so they would be less quick to pinpoint the source of the gunfire."

"Oh, wow!"

"You could never be connected with me."

"Even so. I could see about the car, maybe. No. No, look you leveled with me. I'll level with you."

"Yes?"

"I wouldn't do anything to get in your way. I can see what you're doing and I can dig it, but I can't participate. Do you understand?"

"Of course."

"I suppose it's a cop-out on my part, but I would have to do that, to cop out. I wouldn't get in your way."

"You'd feel no moral imperative to inform anyone in authority?"

"Are you serious? Man, I would never fink. I'm not going to kill Drury, maybe that's my own personal hang-up, but I wouldn't run out and save his life, either."

"That's interesting." Dorn said. "You are not part of the solution."

"I don't follow you."

"Oh?"

Dorn jabbed at the boy's solar plexus, fingers extended and rigid. He drew his hand back and chopped gently at the side of the boy's neck. Gently. He did not kill him.

"You must be part of the problem," he said.

"It's going to be a bad summer," she said. "Not so much because of Drury. You know, that's the thing about something like this. This assassination. It gets all the attention, and everybody takes

47

a set on it, but there are so many other things going on. Did you hear about what happened in Portland?"

"No."

"In Oregon. Not in Maine. God, isn't that weird? There's violence in Portland and you can't even guess which Portland. It happened yesterday. The pigs just broke into a Panther hangout and everybody started blasting away. Three cops killed and five Panthers."

"This was yesterday?"

"Yes. It's just obvious, isn't it? Somebody sent the order down, get the Panthers. And all the cops in the country figure it's open season. It has to be a conspiracy. The Establishment decided to get rid of the Panthers and that's how they're doing it."

He looked at her thoughtfully. "It might be less clear-cut," he suggested.

"How do you figure that?"

"Well, just as a hypothesis. Suppose one man acting by himself called the Portland police. Anonymously. To give them some sort of tip. That there was a cache of heroin at a certain address. That there were armed burglars inside. Anything. And suppose the man then called the Panther house and said the police were on their way with orders to shoot everyone dead. Enter police with guns drawn into room filled with armed Panthers. Result—instant bloodshed."

"My God."

"You're probably right that there is a police conspiracy, but even in the absence of one—"

"I never thought of it that way." Wide blue eyes. "Oh, Miles, that's scary!"

"It's the sort of thing that could happen."

"And I thought I was paranoid before. I don't know about this summer, I really don't. My father wants me to go home to Connecticut. I could hang around here. There are always empty beds in the dormitories during summer session. I can't even concentrate on the choices because of everything that keeps happening. I think about leaving the country. That's what we all talk about. Just getting out of here. This country is on a death trip and I just want to get off."

The speakers' platform was 80 yards from the window of the chemistry lab. There was no wind to speak of. The lab was on the third floor of the building, the top floor, and the slight downward angle was easily allowed for.

There was not much in the way of security. A half-dozen state troopers with high-powered rifles. A handful of obvious plainclothesmen. Enough for his purposes.

("The White Hope. A lot of people say that someone like that does more harm than good.")

When it was time, he moved quickly. He propped the inert Burton Weldon on a chair in front of the window. He had previously opened the window a foot and a half. Now he drew the shade. He crouched behind Weldon, leaned the boy forward a little, put his arms around the slender body, and settled the barrel of the deer rifle on the window ledge.

(". . . . and so the third night he goes to bed in the White House and when he wakes up in the morning he's not J. Lowell Drury anymore, he's Hubert Humphrey.")

A four-power scope. Sighting easily, the cross hairs finding their target.

("I like Drury. I see him on television and I like him.")

Rugged New England features seen through the scope. Face animated, beaming, self-confident.

("But you wonder if the country would be any worse off without him?" "Right. And I can't see how it would.")

He gave the trigger an easy squeeze, popped Drury's skull half an inch above the bridge of his nose. He fired off the rest of the clip, his fingers agile through the sheer gloves, working the bolt between shots, aiming over the crowd, hitting no one. The clip was empty before anyone began returning his fire. He fastened Weldon's hands on the gun, leaned him further forward, and scurried back toward the door. The gunfire began before he was out of the room and was still going on when he cleared the last flight of stairs.

In the bus terminal in Albany a man wanted to talk about Drury. Veins showed on his cheekbones. He wore green workclothes and carried a glossy black lunch bucket.

"About time someone got that sonofabitch. For my money he was asking for it. He was a Commie, you know."

"I didn't know that."

"It wasn't generally known. But I take an interest in these

49

things, see. I'm at the Vets' Post and we get speakers who give you the inside story. Card-carrying Commie. Take my word for it."

"We were talking about Drury again last night, Miles. It's just fantastic the way the same people who said the worst things about him are turning him into a saint."

"You can't be a saint without martyrdom."

"Is that all it is? I think there's more to it than that. Martin Luther King was a saint even before he was shot."

"More people knew it afterward."

"But look at Kennedy. Either Kennedy. I remember when I heard about Dallas. What I was doing, everything. I remember it so completely."

"Everybody does."

"I was like eleven years old. My father hated Kennedy. He had all those jokes about Jackie being a nymphomaniac and the Pope moving into the White House. But after Dallas it was as if he'd never had an unkind thought about the man. He even bought this terrible oil painting of Kennedy and Jackie and the two children, it looked as though it had been painted by numbers, and he wanted to hang it in the living room. My mother wouldn't stand for it. They actually had a fight about it, if you can believe it.

"And then when it happened to Bobby. That was something I really felt happening in myself. We were all for McCarthy. My friends and I, I mean. My father was busy being a Republican again, he would say things like Bobby wasn't anything like the man his brother was. Completely forgetting how he'd felt about his brother in the beginning. But a lot of kids I knew were in the New Hampshire campaign for McCarthy, and we all had it down that Bobby was this vicious calculating opportunist with no principles. And then he died, and it was amazing the way we all went through the identical changes. All of a sudden he was really something, he was a man who could have saved the country. He dug the new politics and he identified with blacks and poor people and at the same time he got across to working people the way McCarthy never could. And we looked at each other and wondered why the fuck it took a bullet to teach us that."

50

"And it's like that with Drury?"

"Uh-huh. You can't help thinking that he might have been somebody, that he might have done something."

"Death supplies time and distance, Jocelyn. It improves most people."

"I keep hating myself for what I said to you. For thinking he wasn't important. Maybe he wasn't, maybe I was right then, and this is just death improving him. I really don't know. But I wish—"

"You have nothing to blame yourself for. You didn't aim the gun, you didn't pull the trigger."

"I know."

"None of the words you spoke to me, none of the thoughts you had, had the slightest thing to do with anything that happened in Maine."

"Oh, I know that."

SEVEN

In New York he stayed at a Times Square hotel under his own name. Each morning he breakfasted at a coffee shop on the corner and read *The New York Times*. Now and then an item would prompt him to nod or to shake his head. Occasionally he would smile.

Several times he went to the microfilm room of the New York Public Library. He liked to go there around noon when the steps outside the building were thick with young people eating lunch out of paper bags and listening to transistor radios. The strip of earth between the sidewalk and the library front was densely planted with tulips and grape hyacinths, the latter just starting to show gray death in their rich blue color. Someone had spray-painted *Free the Panthers* on one of the lions guarding the entrance.

He would sit for hours at a little desk running selected back issues of the *Times* through a large viewer. There were two attendants, a starched and virginal young woman given to white blouses and dark skirts and a loose-limbed boy with abundant curls. Both performed the same quick silent service, bringing him box after box of microfilm cartridges. They were remarkably obliging.

He was constantly amazed that all of this should be made available to him. That he could walk in unannounced, offer no explanation, pay no fee, and not merely make use of the library's resources but be so well served in the process. One day, descending the steps, passing between the stone lions, he wondered what use would be made of the building after the movement had consolidated its position.

Emil Karnofsky lived in a large Edwardian apartment building on Central Park West in the Seventies. There were three doormen working eight-hour shifts around the clock. When a doorman broke for a meal or to use the lavatory, one of the porters relieved him. All guests were announced by the doorman, and no one was admitted to the building until the doorman received the tenant's permission over the intercom system. Two television sets in the lobby monitored the two passenger elevators. The freight elevator was operated by a porter.

Parking was permitted on one side of Central Park West on Mondays, Wednesdays, and Fridays, on the other side on Tuesdays, Thursdays, and Saturdays. Accordingly, several tenants had provided one of the doormen with keys to their cars and had arranged that he move their cars as the regulations dictated. This occupied the doorman for almost an hour each morning, during which time a porter took over his duties.

The building was several stories taller than either of the structures adjoining it.

Karnofsky's apartment was on the tenth floor. He had occupied it without interruption since before the war and remained there after the departure of his children and the death, five years ago, of his wife. A Negro named William Tompkins lived in the apartment and served as Karnofsky's chauffeur, valet, and body-guard. A woman—Dorn did not learn her name—came three times a week to clean the apartment.

Karnofsky was a diabetic. The disease had manifested itself in his late fifties and was controlled with diet and insulin. He had suffered a mild coronary thrombosis in 1957 and had made a complete recovery. He had since given up whiskey and cigars, although he occasionally drank a small cognac before retiring. This he rarely did before two in the morning, spending late hours reading on a wide range of subjects, including the political history of Great Britain during the Industrial Revolution, a topic on which he was an acknowledged authority. He was an early riser. He had been notoriously faithful to his wife during her lifetime and had remained celibate since her death. Every Sunday he was visited by all or some of his grandchildren.

William Tompkins had been with Karnofsky for almost twelve years. For the past fifteen months he had been having an affair with a woman who lived on West 85th Street near Riverside Drive. The woman was married but separated from her husband. She had two small children. Tompkins visited her only during the day, at an hour when Karnofsky was in his office in the Kent-Walker Building and the woman's children were at school. On Tuesday nights he played bridge in Greenwich Village, returning around midnight before his employer was ready to retire. Every Thursday night he visited his widowed mother in Astoria, leaving in time to have dinner with her and returning around 11 o'clock.

None of this was particularly hard for Dorn to learn.

At various times while he was in New York, Dorn read the following items in the *Times* while eating breakfast:

"Calling for 'a spirit of unity and trust in a time of grave division,' the President repeated his appeal for a suspension of political extremism as a memorial to J. Lowell Drury. 'He was a man who knew full well the folly of implacable extremism,' he said of the late senator, 'and if we are to honor his memory . . .'"

". . . sharply criticized Vice-President Henry M. Theodore's recent diatribe on campus dissent and demanded that the White House immediately repudiate the Vice-President's rhetoric . . ."

". . . said that 'Even a man like Drury would be safe in Louisiana. We do things different down here.' He added cryptically, 'I wouldn't be the first person to say something about chickens coming home to roost.' Pressed for further elucidation, he remarked that 'People in this part of the country know what I'm talking about, and the rest of them . . .'"

". . . *thunderous applause from a crowd that filled the auditorium to capacity and overflowed into the street. 'I cannot be a
spectator at the crucifixion of the world's mightiest nation upon
a cross of riot and anarchy. I will not, and you true Americans
shall not, stand idly by while the Statue of Liberty is fitted for
a crown of thorns by the serpents nestled in her own bosom.
John Lowell Drury attempted to make his peace with those very
vipers of the left. But men of good will cannot make peace with
the Devil. John Lowell Drury played with the vipers of the left.
John Lowell Drury learned too late that even he was not immune
to their poison.'*

"*Generally conceded to be an easy victor in his November bid
for reelection, the popular Indiana governor has increasingly
turned his oratorical guns from state to national issues. In response to speculation that . . .*"

Dorn favored the first three items with a nod, and gave the
last a quick smile of recognition.

One night Dorn went to a movie on Times Square. On the
way back to his hotel a young woman emerged from a doorway
and beckoned to him. He stopped to see what she wanted.

She said, "You want some sweet brown sugar, lover? I'll fuck
you, I'll suck you, anything you want."

"Oh, no," Dorn said firmly, then softened it with a smile.
"No," he repeated. "I'm far too old for that."

"You ain't too old," she said as he turned away. "Bet I make
you feel young again."

He walked away.

"Motherfucker!" she called after him.

He walked back to his hotel and went to sleep. In the morning
he went to Central Park and familiarized himself with some of
the paths. He saw a woman feeding bread crumbs to the pigeons.
She seemed to have purchased a bag for that purpose. He thought
that it was nice of her to do this, and was reminded of an item
he had read reporting that the Board of Aldermen somewhere
had appropriated funds for a program designed to eradicate
pigeons by feeding them with a chemical which would interfere
with their reproductive processes. They would lay eggs, but the
eggs would not have shells. This was heralded as humane. Dorn
wondered why. The pigeons were to be eradicated—terminated,

Dorn thought—because they had a propensity for shitting on statues and the steps of public buildings.

It is in the nature of pigeons, Dorn thought, to shit on statues.

It occurred to him that this woman might be feeding such a chemical to the pigeons. She might even be poisoning them. It was impossible to say with certainty.

He took a taxi back to his hotel, packed, checked out. He caught an afternoon flight to Charleston and a bus to Willow Falls.

"How was New York?"

"Exhausting," he told her. In German he recited its faults. German was a good language for finding fault. "It is, in the first place, impossible to breathe the air or drink the water. There is a trash receptacle on every corner, but no one seems to have informed the public of its function. Consequently the streets and sidewalks are strewn with garbage. One cannot walk a block without being accosted by several panhandlers, perhaps a third of whom were better dressed than I. All of the taxis seem to be permanently off-duty. Everyone is shrunken and sullen-faced. No one smiles. I see no reason why anyone should."

"I was going to say I wished I could have gone along. But you don't make it sound very wonderful."

"It was not very wonderful at all. Be glad you were here. Anyone who goes unnecessarily to New York is flirting with commitment to a mental hospital. The city itself is a mental hospital, all patients and no staff."

"Oh, poor Miles."

"I survived. Actually I spent almost all of my time at the Public Library. An excellent institution. And, perhaps because I hated the city so much, I managed to get an impressive amount of research done in a week's time."

"I wish you would give me at least a hint of what this project is about."

"In due time. You see, I know that if I talk about it, I won't get around to doing it."

"I don't mean to bug you." When he squinted at the idiom, meaningless in German, she translated it.

"But you don't bug me," he said.

"At least you won't have to go back to New York again, will you?"

55

"I sincerely hope I will never have to go back there," he said.

"You're a good cook," she said. "This is really delicious. I don't know how to cook anything."

"It's not hard to learn."

"Do you give cooking lessons? I could afford them, now that my German lessons are free."

"I learn more from you than I teach you, Jocelyn."

She put her fork down, raised her face slowly to his. She spoke to him with her face. *If you want,* her face said. *If you would like it, I too would like it. Truly. But you're the one who must decide.*

"It's warm," he said. "I'll open a window."

EIGHT

Less than a week after his return from New York, Dorn packed a suitcase and rode a bus to Charleston. From Charleston he flew on Delta Airlines to New Orleans. The name on his ticket was not one he had used before. He used that name again to register at a medium-priced hotel in the Quarter. In his room he unpacked his suitcase and placed his clothes in the bureau and closet. He took the *Sanitized* wrapper off the toilet seat and raised the seat. He unwrapped one of the water tumblers, drew a glass of water, drank some of it—it tasted of chlorine—and set the half-empty glass on top of the dresser. He took off the bedspread, got into bed, rumpled the bedclothing briefly, dented the pillow with his head, and got out of bed again. He closed the blinds and turned up the air conditioning.

On his way out of the room he dropped the *Do Not Disturb* sign onto the doorknob. He knew several ways to lock a door from the inside while being on the outside. None of them worked with this particular type of lock. There was a transom, but the desirability of having the door locked from the inside did not seem to him to outweigh the probable consequences of being

56

seen crawling through his own transom, nor did he much like the idea of trying to crawl back in again. Nor, for that matter, did a broken leg lend itself to his plans.

He stopped at the hotel coffee shop, ate a quick breakfast, signed the chit with his current name and room number. He kept his room key, and left the hotel through the coffee shop's street entrance to avoid passing the desk.

A taxi took him back to the airport. He had earlier reserved a seat under another new name on an American Airlines flight to Kennedy Airport, which he still thought of as Idlewild. ("*You can't be a saint without martyrdom.*") His flight was called for boarding ten minutes after he arrived at the airport.

He enjoyed the flight. One of the stewardesses reminded him in some indefinable way of Jocelyn, although there was no actual physical resemblance. He ate an adequate meal and had several cups of tea.

He spent a good deal of time thinking about Emil Karnofsky, but thought about other things as well.

Although he had long since destroyed all of the capsule biographies Heidigger had given him, his memory of them was eidetic.

Emil Karnofsky. Director, National Brotherhood of Clothing Workers. Member, national board, AFL-CIO. Jew. First major labor leader to take antiwar position. Union membership chiefly black, Puerto Rican. Respected by colleagues but regarded as New York Jew leftist. Termination advised to foster solidarity in labor circles. Strongly recommend termination via natural causes or accident. If unavoidably otherwise, political motivation must not be suggested. Age: 77. Widower. Three children, eight grand-children . . .

His flight was stacked in a holding pattern over Kennedy for almost two hours, to the dismay of most of Dorn's fellow passengers, at least one of whom seemed to hold the stewardesses personally accountable. Dorn was unbothered by the delay. He had allowed for it.

A telephone conversation:

"Hello, Mr. Tompkins?"

"No, this is Emil Karnofsky. Did you wish to speak with Mr. Tompkins?"

"I'd like to speak to Mr. William Tompkins, yes."

"I'm sorry, but Mr. Tompkins is not in now. I expect him in about two hours, perhaps sooner. If you would care to—"

"Do you have a number where he can be reached?"

"May I ask who is calling?"

"This is Sgt. Bernard Cleary attached to the 47th police precinct in Astoria."

"Oh, I hope nothing's—"

"Do you have a number where Mr. Tompkins can be reached?"

"Yes, I do. Excuse me a moment. Yes. Sergeant?"

"Yes."

"The number is 868 . . . ."

Another telephone conversation:

"Hello?"

"Mr. William Tompkins, please."

"Right. Just a minute. Bill? Take your time, it's a man."

"Hello?"

"Is this William Tompkins? Mr. Tompkins, this is Sgt. Bernard Cleary . . . ."

Another telephone conversation:

"Hello?"

"Mr. Karnofsky, this is—"

"Yes, Bill, I was waiting for you to call. It's your mother?"

"They just called me. They—"

"Are you all right, Bill?"

"Yes, sir. I'll be all right. She—"

"Take your time, Bill."

"Someone broke in and beat her real bad, Mr. Karnofsky. Some crazy man. A woman like that, a sweet woman like that, to break into her house and beat her—"

"Is she all right?"

"They got her down at the hospital. They don't know, you know, how she's . . . . how she's gonna—"

"Go straight there, Bill. Take the car. Unless you don't think you should drive."

"No cab's going to Astoria at this hour. I'm all right now, Mr. Karnofsky. And driving calms me. I relax myself driving whereas I worry when someone else drives me."

"Go ahead, then. And don't worry about me. I want you to

stay with your mother as long as she needs you, as long as you feel you want to be with her."

"You're a good man, Mr. Karnofsky. You are good to me."

"Oh, now."

"I don't like to leave you, Mr. Karnofsky."

"Am I a child afraid of the dark? I can take my own shot, I can turn off my own lights, and in the morning I can make my own breakfast. And if I have anywhere to go tomorrow or the next day or as long as it takes, Bill, I can call downtown, and they will send me a car and a driver. Now go to your mother and stop wasting your time talking to an old man. . . .

Another telephone conversation:

"Hello?"

"Hello, is this Rebecca Warriner?"

"Yes."

"Rebecca, my name is Milton Burdett. Howard Kleinman said I ought to give you a call."

"Howard Kleinman."

"From Kansas City?"

"I guess so."

"He may have just said Howard, I don't—"

"Yeah, right. Be cool on the phone, right?"

"Oh."

"It's okay. Did you, uh, you wanted to come up?"

"I would like that."

"You know the address?"

"Yes, I have it."

"Give me your name again, because the doorman will have to announce you."

"Milton Burdett. With two *t*'s."

"He's not going to spell it, Milton."

"Oh, of course. There won't be any trouble with the doorman, will there? Howard—I didn't know about a doorman."

"Not the way I tip, there won't be, Milton. You come right up. I'm glad you called, I was lonely."

Dorn rode the elevator to the fourteenth floor. He rang the bell of Apartment 14-D, and the door was opened almost immediately by a tall girl with very long black hair. She was wearing skintight black slacks and a yellow sweater. She had large breasts.

She said, "Milton? Come in, let's get acquainted. Do I call you Milton or Milt?"

"Milton," Dorn said. "I don't have much time."

"Oh, that's a shame. I thought we could have a good long time together."

Dorn found it remarkable that she could invest the words with such sincerity.

"I have . . . a special thing," he said.

"Uh-huh."

He drew a pair of fifty-dollar bills from his wallet and handed them to her. She reached out for the money, then drew her hand back.

"I don't take beatings," she said. "Except with a cloth belt that I have. Or being tied up, I don't do that."

"I wouldn't ask you to do anything like that."

"Well, maybe you could tell me in front what it is you want me to do."

"In front?"

"Now, I mean."

"Oh. I understand. I would like you to take off all your clothing."

"So far we're in business. And?"

"And I want you to do jumping jacks."

"Huh?"

"Jumping jacks," he said happily. "Have you never done jumping jacks?" He stood with his feet together and his hands at his sides, then sprang, and flung his arms up so that he wound up with his feet spread and his hands touching above his head. He returned to the original posture, then repeated the whole process. "Jumping jacks."

"Oh, sure. Jumping jacks. We used to do that in an exercise class."

"Then you'll do them?"

"I suppose. What'll you be doing while I'm doing jumping jacks?"

"I will sit in that chair," he said, "and I will watch you."

"That's it?" He nodded. "Groovy," she said, taking the money. "You're nice, Milton."

"And don't talk while you do the jumping jacks."

60

"Anything you say."

He seated himself in the chair. It was quite comfortable. The whole apartment was tastefully furnished. She undressed quickly. He beamed at her. She began doing jumping jacks. He watched her as attentively as he possibly could. Much of his flight time had been devoted to determining what he would ask her to do. It had to be something that involved no disrobing on his part, and no physical contact.

She went on doing jumping jacks and he watched her breasts bounce heroically. After a few moments he stiffened, then slumped in the chair. Eyes closed he said, "You can stop now."

"That was quick."

"Usually I can last longer."

"It's a compliment to my excitingness. You're very sweet, Milton. You want a Coke or something?"

"I have to go."

"Uh-huh. You come and see me next time you're in town, okay? That was lots of fun."

"And good exercise."

"Oh, it certainly was. Keeps me in shape. 'Bye, now."

He walked toward the elevator. When her door closed he doubled back and walked down four flights of stairs. He knocked softly on the door of Apartment 10-H. There was no response. He knocked again, somewhat louder. There was still no response.

He put his ear to the door and listened very carefully. He heard nothing.

There were four locks on the door of Apartment 10-H. One of them took him 30 seconds. The others were somewhat easier. After he had picked the fourth and last lock, he put on his gloves again and wiped the door where he might have touched it. He listened again, very carefully, and let himself inside.

The apartment was dark except for a ten-watt night-light in one hallway. He let his eyes accustom themselves to the dimness. Then he took off his shoes and crept around in his stocking feet until he found Emil Karnofsky's bedroom.

He used a pencil-beam flashlight. Karnofsky was sleeping on his side, clutching his pillow. Sparse gray hair, a prominent nose, a forceful jaw.

He tiptoed to the bedside and stood for a moment, deep in thought. Then he stooped and placed one hand over Karnofsky's mouth while his other sought purchase on the back of the old

61

man's neck. He was gentle, very gentle, taking away the chance of consciousness but being careful not to take away life as well.

He moved around the apartment, making sure the blinds were drawn. Then he turned on the living room lights and carried Karnofsky to the living room. The man did not stir. He went back to the bedroom for the silk dressing gown he had noticed there before. He took it to the living room and got Karnofsky's arms into it.

He stripped himself to the waist, placing his clothing neatly on Karnofsky's couch. From his jacket pocket he took out an eight-inch length of steel pipe wrapped not too thickly with electrical tape. He lifted Karnofsky and propped him against a wall. The man still had not stirred but was breathing regularly.

Dorn smashed his skull with four blows.

It occurred to him as he was doing so that he should have removed his gloves, but no blood got on them, or on his person. He dressed quickly but carefully. Then he went through the apartment room by room, turning lights on as he entered each room and off as he left it. He pulled open drawers, slashed mattresses, knocked books off shelves. He made the greatest mess possible in the shortest amount of time. He found several hundred dollars in a drawer of the bedside table and almost a thousand in the butter compartment of the refrigerator. He added this to the money in his wallet. He removed every picture he came to until he found the one behind which the wall safe was located. He made no attempt to open the wall safe.

When he was through, he turned off the living room light and listened with his ear against the door for several moments. He put the tape-wrapped pipe on the floor near Karnofsky's corpse. He opened the door quietly and let himself out. He climbed four flights of stairs to Rebecca Warriner's floor and rang for the elevator. On the way down he smiled a lot and did not look at the camera.

The doorman treated him to a smirk and hailed him a taxi. He took the cab to the Hotel Somerset. He waited while it drove off, then walked a block in the opposite direction and took a taxi to Penn Station. There he picked up a third taxi and rode out to Kennedy Airport. The driver talked endlessly of baseball.

He waited over an hour before his flight was called. Takeoff was on schedule, and arrival at New Orleans was 12 minutes early. Dorn dozed on the plane and smiled at memories of Rebecca Warriner. Not of her long black hair, not of her bouncing breasts, but of her dialogue, and of her immutable poise. Why were his best stories ones he could tell no living ear?

A taxi from the airport let him off within a block of his hotel. He bought a paper and read it as he ate breakfast in his hotel's coffee shop. He went through the lobby to the elevator and rode up to his room. As far as he could tell, no one had been in it since he had left. He showered and put on clean clothes. He turned the *Do Not Disturb* sign around so that it read *Maid Please Make Up This Room As Soon As Possible*. On his way out he left his room key at the desk.

He slept for four hours in a movie theater, waking when some fool put a hand on his leg. He left the theater and bought an evening paper. There were several items he found noteworthy, but nothing about Karnofsky. He stopped at a bar and nursed a glass of wine through the six o'clock newscast. There was a brief item to the effect that Emil Karnofsky had been beaten to death during a burglary of his New York apartment.

He had dinner at an excellent restaurant near his hotel and walked over to Preservation Hall to listen to the music, but the place was crowded and he did not stay long. He went back to his hotel and read for a few hours before going to sleep.

He read the story in the New Orleans morning newspaper. The content was about as he had expected. He went looking for a drugstore with a pay telephone.

A long-distance telephone call:

"Hello?"

"Hello."

"I hoped you'd call. We liked your timing but the touch was heavy, don't you think?"

"What?"

"You're good on the calendar but—"

"Let me talk, I'm too upset to listen."

"Upset?"

"I thought this was a solo, damn it."

"Repeat."

"I said, damn it, that I thought I had a six-time exclusive."

"You do."

63

"Then what happened to Case Two?"

Pause.

"Are you there, damn it?"

"Yes. You did not do Case Two?"

"I have been in—oh, shit on it. I have been in the largest account in Case Three's district—do you read?"

"In Case *Three's* district?"

"Yes."

"I read."

"I have been here since yesterday morning. I have been looking around Case Three while waiting to conclude Case Two. Then I picked up a newspaper. Then I picked up a telephone."

"Christ."

"You didn't know about this?"

"Of course not. Christ. Can I get back to you?"

"No."

"Then get back to me. An hour."

Another long-distance telephone call.

"Hello. We didn't do Case Two."

"Certain?"

"Certain. I checked all possibilities. We did not do Case Two."

"Then who in the hell did?"

"Our supposition is the printed version is real."

"I don't believe it."

"Neither did I. How clean is your line?"

"Could be anonymously dirty. Drugstore."

"Shit." In rapid Serbo-Croat: "It smells. A commercial touch on the black's night out? And a call to send him snipe hunting? But I think it was commercial. They would know the schedule. And it was not a snipe hunt."

"Repeat last."

"I checked this six ways. They were good to begin with and had fantastic luck. The snipe hunt was honest. The black hen was plucked. The snipe call was straight merchandise."

"Incredible."

"Absolutely."

"Their good luck. And—"

"And shit luck for us, damn it to hell."

"Yes."

"Because after all that they scored small. They tossed and

didn't clean. Nickels and dimes. Christ damn it to fucking hell."

"I would never have done it heavy."

"Of course not. In and out. Stop the clock and go away. No bad smell."

"Exactly."

"So instead of a light touch it winds up being heavy and smelling to high heaven."

"And this after a stinking week casing it."

"Too long on this line. Anything more?"

"No. Shit."

He spent the rest of the day in New Orleans, doing various things. One of the places he visited was a wildlife museum, where he examined row after row of glass cases filled with dead birds. Several of them were specimens of extinct species. He got half-way through the display when he was overcome by a feeling of utter revulsion. He left the building as quickly as he could, certain that the sight of one more dead bird would make him vomit.

The next day he took a bus to Baton Rouge. He paid two dollars and twenty-five cents to take a one-hour tour of the city on a sight-seeing bus. Like everyone else, he had a camera. He visited, among other places, the State Capitol, the Governor's Mansion, and the campus of Louisiana State University. When the tour ended he took another bus back to New Orleans and checked out of his hotel, settling his bill in cash. Then he flew again to Charleston and took the bus to Willow Falls. All that day, on the plane and on all the buses, he kept thinking of those display cases with their dead birds. He hardly thought at all of Karnofsky, or of William Tompkins's mother.

NINE

For several weeks Dorn spent the greater portion of his time in his house in Willow Falls. The weather turned quite warm, and the house was not air conditioned, but Dorn did not mind the heat. In recent years he had found himself less capable of enduring extreme cold temperatures, but hot weather had never bothered him.

Now and then he took a bus somewhere for all or part of a day, but he never stayed away overnight during this period. He went various places, observed various people, read various books and newspapers and periodicals, and spoke at various times on the telephone.

While he was thus engaged, several things happened here and there across the nation. In Chevy Chase, Maryland, Senator Willard Cosgriff (Rep., Colo.) lost control of his automobile and plowed into a concrete bridge support. He was killed instantly. Autopsy revealed an unusually high concentration of alcohol in his bloodstream. Senator Cosgriff had been a sharp critic of the administration's war policy.

A bomb exploded in the main Chicago police station, killing three police officers engaged in clerical duties. Investigation failed to yield any positive clues, although an anonymous letter on behalf of the African Revolutionary Movement took credit for the bombing. The letter contained circumstantial information on the incident which had been withheld from publication. No organization named the African Revolutionary Movement had been previously known to the authorities, in either Chicago or Washington.

In response to the threat of a disturbance on the Bloomington campus of the University of Indiana, Governor James Danton Rhodine threw a cordon of National Guard troops around the campus. Simultaneously, forty-three student leaders were quietly arrested and charged with crimes ranging from possession of marijuana to fomenting rebellion and civil disorders. Bail was denied to all but five of the students. There was no subsequent disturbance on the campus, and the troops were called off after two days without a rock being hurled or a shot fired. Governor Rhodine's several speeches and press conferences, in which he spoke of "nipping Red rebellion in the bud," received extensive national press and television coverage.

A Louis Harris poll on 1972 presidential preferences for the first time included the name of James Danton Rhodine.

In Detroit, auto workers marching in support of the administration's Indo-China policy clashed with peace demonstrators in a battle that raged for eight blocks on Woodward Avenue. Police units, ordered into action immediately by Mayor Walter Isaac James, later drew fire for their lackadaisical attitude in restoring order. Twenty-three auto workers and seventy-six peace marchers received hospital treatment, and two peace marchers subsequently died as the result of injuries sustained in the fray. Spokesmen for each side charged the other with deliberate organized provocation.

The cumulative death toll across the nation during this period of time included fourteen police officers and thirty-one persons identified as members or sympathizers of the Black Panther Party.

In Buffalo, New York, the headquarters of a branch of the Weatherman faction of Students for a Democratic Society was raided during the night by persons unknown. The Weathermen had opened this headquarters with an eye toward organizing white working-class support in Buffalo's predominantly Polish East Side. The office was sacked, mimeograph equipment destroyed, and two Weathermen beaten to death.

The Secret Service investigated over twenty-five hundred threats on the lives of the President and Vice-President.

The baby robins, still uncertain fliers, began leaving their nest for longer periods of time.

Dorn saw Jocelyn almost every day, except for those days when he had business out of town. On afternoons when she did not visit him he found himself stalking uncertainly around the house and yard, picking things up and putting them down, waiting impatiently for her.

He held long conversations with her when she visited him, and longer conversations with her in his mind when she did not.

Jocelyn, you know nothing of the man I have been or even of the man I am. Jocelyn, I first killed a man when I was seventeen years old. I killed him because he was a Serb and I was a Croat. At the time this seemed sufficient reason. By the time I was your age, Jocelyn, I literally could not count the men I had killed. I did not know their number.

Often he read poetry. Blake. Yeats. Rilke. Schiller. Eliot.

"I should have been a pair of ragged claws. . . .
"I shall wear white flannel trousers and walk upon the beach.
"I have heard the mermaids singing, each to each.
"I do not think that they will sing to me. . . ."

"I brought a friend to see you," she said one morning. "I hope you don't mind."

She held the friend in her arms, small and black, with white forepaws and a white tip to his tail.

"The notorious Vertigo," he said. "I had begun to question the fact of his existence, as if he were God and I a Catholic adolescent. Welcome to my unworthy house, Vertigo."

They sat with cups of tea. Dorn poured a saucer of milk for Vertigo, who sniffed it and walked away from it.

"Vertigo," she said. "That's not at all polite."

"That is the strength of cats. They are not amenable to bribery."

The cat walked from room to room, investigating. Jocelyn began to talk of James Danton Rhodine. This was not surprising to Dorn. He had noticed that more and more people were beginning to talk of James Danton Rhodine. The man projected vigor, imagination, strength. He knew the right words and spoke them with the ring of conviction. He talked of progress through a return to traditional American values. He praised the spirit of God-fearing American workers and farmers, who toiled for their bread and lived decent honest lives. He railed at the vipers of the left who would divide the country. He quoted Lincoln's observation about a house divided. The vipers of the left, he suggested, were moved to divide and conquer.

"I just don't know," she said, her face troubled. "Everybody says he's a reactionary, and I guess he is. But—"

"Yes?"

"Sometimes I can't help feeling that some of the things he says make sense."

"What do your friends say?"

"Everybody hates him. You know, 'fascist bastard.' He's an obvious racist. He doesn't come right out with it like that red-neck Guthrie. But it's there. There's a phrase he uses. 'The speckled band of subversion.' "

"I thought that was a reference to Sherlock Holmes. He calls radicals 'vipers of the left,' and the 'speckled band' was a snake in a Conan Doyle story."

"I know. But first he'll talk about the black nationalists, and then he'll talk about radical college students, and then he'll use this 'speckled band' thing. Like speckled black and white. That's what I get from it."

"I see. A subtly racist remark."

"That's it, Miles. He's subtle. And he's so great on television. There was one speech I saw, I only caught the tail end of it, and there wasn't a thing he said that I especially agreed with, but when he finished, I don't know, I felt like standing up and singing 'God Bless America.' I felt like marching."

"Interesting."

"I hear people I know say, 'I don't like him, but he has some good ideas.' Once I heard a friend of my father's say that about Hitler."

Dorn smiled. "Ah. Hitler did have some good ideas, you know. The German people went to him as an alternative to chaos. And he put a stop to inflation, and increased employment, and raised the standard of living, and ended civil disorder, and reversed the terms of Versailles. And—"

"You make it sound—"

"And then, when he had evidently saved the German people from chaos, he went on to create for them the most nearly total chaos the world has ever known. He launched an impossible and unnecessary war. He guided the war so as to make utter defeat inevitable. He slaughtered millions. Millions. He destroyed all that he had created along with all that had existed before him. The savior from chaos turned himself into the supreme nihilist. But he had some good ideas."

"Do you think—"

"A wild exaggeration on my part," he said. "After all, this is America."

There was the noise of a small struggle outside, and unfamiliar sounds of pain. Dorn rushed out the front door. Jocelyn was close behind him. The cat was in a bed of irises by the side of the front steps, killing something.

"Oh, Vertigo!"

Dorn stooped for a closer look.

"Is it a mouse?"

He took hold of the cat by the nape of the neck and retrieved its tiny victim.

"It's a bird," he said. "A young robin."

"Oh, *no!*" She stood over the cat, her face drawn with anguish. "Vertigo, you bad cat! How could you do it? Oh, you bad, bad cat!"

Dorn had released his hold on the cat's neck. Vertigo looked up, puzzled, as the girl wailed at him. He stood still while she slapped him twice across his face. Then, baffled, he darted off into the bushes.

"Oh, God," she said. She was shuddering. "How could he do that? How did he get out?"

"It was my fault. There were windows open. It did not occur to me that he might leave."

"No, I should have thought. He never did anything like that before. He's always been a good cat, a wonderful cat. He never even puts out his claws. How could he do that? Is the poor thing—"

There was life in the bird that he held in his hands, but it was terribly mauled. "I'm afraid it's dead," he said gently. "Go in and sit down. I'll bury it."

He walked to the garage, giving the bird's neck a quick snap as he walked. He got his trowel and buried the bird in a flower bed.

She was on the front steps, calling to the cat. "He won't come," she said. "Oh! I never hit him before. He didn't know what was happening, and now I don't know where he is and he won't come when I call him."

"Come inside," he said. "He'll be back."

"How do you know?"

"He wants to go off and consider what's happened to him. But he'll be back."

In the living room she said, "Was it one of our birds?" They went together to the kitchen window. One of the baby robins was absent from the nest. She began to cry, her shoulders heaving, tears flowing freely. Awkwardly he put an arm around her shoulders. She pressed her face against his chest and cried for a long time. He felt as though something was breaking inside his chest. At last her sobbing stopped and she sighed deeply. He released her. She took a step backward, turning her face from him.

"I'm such a child," she said.

He said nothing.

"I don't understand how he could do it. I named him Vertigo because he has this height thing. I never met a cat like that before. He has to work up his courage to jump down from my bed. How could he get into the nest?"

"They've been leaving the nest. But they don't fly well. They're easy to catch, even for clumsy cats. The parent birds would have driven Vertigo away, but evidently they were off on other errands."

"We watched those birds grow up. And then he—"

"You can't blame him. It's the nature of cats to kill birds."

"But how would he know to do it?"

"As he knows to arch his back at dogs, land on four feet, and clean himself."

"Damn it, he doesn't *have* to catch birds! I feed him twice a day. I spend more on *his* meals than—"

"What do you feed him?"

"Cat food."

"What does it contain?"

"Everything he needs, protein, vitamins—"

"I mean the composition?"

"Everything. Beef and liver and chicken and fish and—oh!"

"Don't, Jocelyn."

But she began to cry again, and this time he did not attempt to comfort her. She covered her face with her hands and wept. "It's so wrong," she sobbed. "Why does everything have to eat everything else? Why?"

"Why must cats eat birds?"

"Why?"

"Why do we cry for the birds eaten by cats, when we do not cry for the worms eaten by birds? And why does all our knowledge of the balance of nature and the survival of the fittest do nothing to stop our tears?"

"It is so awful, Miles."

He ached for her. She was getting a quick glimpse of Hell from a new perspectiv   nd there were no words he could speak to blur her vision.

The cat's return to the house was as unremarked as his exit. All at once he was there, in the living room.

"Oh, Vertigo," she cried. She ran to pick him up. He turned, wary of her, but she snatched him up and clutched him to her breasts.

"Oh, poor, poor Vertigo," she said. "I should never have hit you. I didn't think you would come back. My poor baby. My poor sweet baby."

She sat with the cat purring in her lap. Dorn went from room to room, closing windows.

Jocelyn, it's the nature of cats to kill birds. Jocelyn, it is my nature to kill men. Vertigo and I are assassins. It is our nature. And to live in accordance with one's nature is to make one's peace with destiny.

"Tyger, tyger . . . . did he who made the lamb make thee?" The same hand made both beasts, Jocelyn.

Jocelyn, I go through life with a gun in my hands. But I, Jocelyn, am a gun in the hands of a man named Eric Heidigger. And he in his turn is a gun in an unseen pair of hands. And James Danton Rhodine (who has some good ideas) is part of this chain of guns and hands, but whether he is a gun or a pair of hands or both I do not know.

Why, Jocelyn, do we grieve so much more bitterly for the death of a young animal? Why is the death of a child so infinitely more sorrowful than the death of an adult?

You wept at once for bird and cat. I weep for you.

One evening after dinner she turned suddenly and caught him looking at her, his face open and unguarded.

"Oh, Miles," she said.

He tried to turn his eyes from her. They stayed on her face, her perfect face.

She said, "You must know that I love you."

("I should have been a pair of ragged claws. . . .")

She said, "And you love me. I know you do."

(". . . the mermaids singing . . .")

She said, "I don't have anyone else. Not anymore. When you go out of town—?"

He thought of Rebecca Warriner· *("You're very sweet, Milton. . . . That was lots of fun.")* He thought of the streetwalker.

"No," he said. *("No. I'm far too old for that.")*

Jocelyn, Jocelyn, I am not a lover but a killer. My penis is a rifle spitting bullets into other men's brains, a steel bar that pulps their heads. A knife. A stick of dynamite. A dozen dozen forms of phallic death.

My seed is acid, Jocelyn. The universal solvent that no vessel can contain.

He watched as she stepped purposefully across the room to

him. (*"It's warm. I'll open a window."*) He remained in his armchair, his eyes on the softness of her smile. She seated herself sideways on his lap. He looked down at blue jeans and bare feet. She put her hands on his shoulders and looked into his eyes, and he returned the look.

The warmth, the beauty, the smell of her.

He thought of cats and birds, of worms and men. He touched her leg and looked at his hand upon faded blue denim.

(*". . . ragged claws . . ."*)

"I am an old man."

"You are not old."

"And you are so very young."

She kissed him lightly on the lips. His hands remembered the wounded robin, the tapping of its heart, the weak flutter of crippled wings. She kissed him again, and he drew her to him and tasted her mouth.

"Old. . . ."

"We are the same age, Miles. I have known you for as long as you have known me."

He held her close. She put her arms around his neck, her head in the hollow of his shoulder. He felt a heartbeat and did not know whether it was hers or his own.

(*"Do I dare eat a peach?"*)

"I love you," he said.

"Oh, I know, I know."

"I love you."

He held her. A kitten on his lap, purring. He held her, and his hand moved to cup her breast, to touch her arm, the side of her face.

After a long time she stood up and held out her hands to him. He got to his feet. Her face melted into that warm liquid look he had glimpsed only once before.

(*"You were my teacher, and now you are my friend."*)

They walked arm in arm to the bedroom.

Oh, Jocelyn! Warmth, fire, love. A gun, a knife, a stick of dynamite, a length of steel pipe. Not peace but a sword. Jocelyn! Do I dare?

I will not commit suicide, Jocelyn. I will not leave the country.

He lay on his back, every muscle unstrung, every cell at peace. Her hair brushed his face. He opened his eyes to see her looking down at him.

"Hello, old man."

"Hello."

Her hand reached for him, her fingers curled possessively around his penis. She said, "I have made a discovery, old man. Men are like wine."

"Some turn to vinegar."

"Not the good ones. Oh, if you could see your face."

"How do I look?"

"Proud. Beautiful. Grand. How do I look?"

"Beautiful."

"And a little bit *ausgeshtupped*?"

He laughed, delighted. "But I never taught you that word!"

"Did I get it right?"

"Close enough."

She stretched out at his side. He closed his eyes and learned her body with his hands.

"Miles? What did you say to me the first day?"

"When?"

"You said things in different languages so I would know the sound of each."

"I said nothing of importance."

"What did you say in German?" She swung into a sitting position, legs curled under her. "I knew it! Miles, you're blushing!"

"How did you know?"

"Tell me what you said."

"No."

"Miles!" She turned his face toward hers. "I *knew* it! There was something different about your face when you spoke German. That's why I picked it. Tell me what you said."

"I cannot tell you."

"Say it in German."

"But now you would understand it."

"Miles—"

He said, "*Du hast Haar wie gesponnenes Gold und eine Haut wie warme Milch. Wäre ich nicht über diese Dinge hinaus würde ich Deinen Rock lüften und stundenlang Deinen Schoss küssen.*"

"You devil."

74

He felt a grin spread foolishly on his face.

"Devil!" she repeated. "Of course, I can't be positive what *Schoss* means. Somehow it never came up in our conversations. Dirty old man! Sweet beautiful dirty old man!" She stretched out, lay on her back, parted her thighs. A wanton glow spread on her face. "I don't have a skirt for you to lift. Does that matter very much?"

TEN

William Roy Guthrie.

Three-term governor of Louisiana. Presidential candidate, Free American Party, 1964, 1968. Sectionalist demagogue with minor racist appeal in industrial Midwest. Controlled alcoholic. Insufficient stature and character for national leadership. Political program neopopulist, negative. Termination advised to allow his personal following in the southeast to flow into the movement. Termination of Guthrie must precede termination of Theodore. Thrust may come from black extremist or university radical. This cover should be opaque. Age: 57. Married. No children . . .

When Dorn was in Baltimore,

a young black with an Afro hairstyle thrust a newspaper at him while he was walking down the street. "Read the truth, sir," the boy said.

Dorn had been thinking of something far removed from Baltimore. Far removed, too, from the truth. He blinked, drew back, recovered, and reached to take the paper. It was a tabloid. The headline, bold black type over a red background, shrieked of murder. One of the stories that caught his eye spoke of a nationwide network of concentration camps for blacks.

"What is this?"

"The truth," the boy said, as if by rote. "You won't get it elsewhere, sir. Published by the Black Panther Party. And that's the truth."

Dorn squinted at the upper-right corner. "The price is twenty-five cents?"

"Yes, sir."

Dorn dug out a five-dollar bill. "Interesting," he said. "I could use a dozen of these."

"I'll have to give you some coin—"

"No, keep the change," Dorn said. "Power to the people."

"Right *on!*"

In Chicago, police arrested a seventeen-year-old high school dropout for questioning in connection with the bombing of police headquarters. He was reported to have confessed to participation in the act and to have named several associates in the plot before breaking loose from his captors and hurling himself through a fourth-story window. He died in the fall.

Dorn read several accounts of the incident. In one of these, the reaction of Governor Guthrie was reported as follows:

"In a characteristic gesture, the florid-faced Louisiana governor winked and laid a finger alongside his nose. 'I'll tell you, boys,' he said confidentially, 'it's a good thing we don't get that sort of agitation down in my part of the country. I don't know what-all we might do. We just don't have a window high enough to chuck one of those fellers out of. I guess we'd just have to take him on up to Chicago.' Governor Guthrie went on to cluck at reporters who asked if he were suggesting extralegal action on the part of the Chicago police, or if his words constituted an endorsement of such tactics. 'I don't know why on earth I bother chatting with you boys,' he said in mock exasperation. 'You know you just twist every old thing I say. And you never can tell when I'm cracking jokes with you.'"

In a room in a Holiday Inn in Charlotte, North Carolina, Heidigger was engaged in a spirited analysis of the relative merits of stewardesses on various U.S. airlines. The TWA girls were the best-looking. The ones on American were the best at their work. The ones on Northeast were tough and brassy. On United—

Dorn bathed in the flow of words without attempting to pay

attention to them. He watched Heidigger bounce about, gesturing theatrically with his hands, flashing gold teeth, punctuating his words with a thrust of his cigar. Light glinted off his bald head. The fringe of white hair had not been cut since Dorn had last seen him, and it gave him the look of a mad scientist in a horror film. The white lunatic fringe, Dorn thought.

". . . . their wonderfully transitory quality, Miles. For the length of the flight they hover over you, suffer your abuse, indulge your whims. Then the plane lands, and you never see them again. In retrospect their faces merge into a single face, their bodies into a single body. Do you know what they resemble? They are like whores. Instead of cunt they give you coffee."

If there is a Day of Judgment, Dorn thought, what would weigh most heavily against him was not the crimes he had committed but that he actually liked Eric Heidigger. He had been thinking about this for some time and had been unable to settle on the reason why it was so. He did not like to believe it was because Heidigger so obviously appreciated his talent. One often enough liked people for lesser reasons than that, but it nevertheless seemed to him that his affection for Heidigger—that was what it was, affection—should have a rather deeper motivation.

Psychoanalysis could perhaps furnish an explanation, he thought, and smiled at the image. Suppose he had stretched out on Greenspan's couch that day and spoken truth instead of fiction. *I am an assassin, Doctor, and I am concerned that I feel a genuine affection for my employer.* He grinned, imagining Greenspan tugging at his little beard and nodding, nodding, nodding.

"Well," Heidigger said. "To more explosive matters, wouldn't you say? I have what you ordered."

"Good."

"It's under the bed. A little package for you. Could you get it? But please don't drop it."

"If it's what I asked for, Eric, you could drop it off the Empire State Building and nothing would happen. Unless it hit some poor fool on the head."

"Merely a joke, Miles. It is as you ordered it. Although we could have engineered something to specifications if you had permitted it."

"I prefer to do my own assembling."

"And wisely, I think. Trust your own craft."

"I prefer it."

"Under the bed, then. The far end. I would get it myself, but my stomach gets in the way when I bend over. Hence I do so as infrequently as possible."

Dorn felt distinctly uncomfortable kneeling on the floor and fumbling under Heidigger's bed for the parcel. In his mind's eye he envisioned Heidigger moving up behind him, putting a pistol to the back of his neck. One of the negative aspects of his profession was that one was not only instinctively cautious in times of danger but was quite as apprehensive in perfectly safe situations.

The parcel was half the size of a cigar box. It was wrapped in birthday wrapping paper and tied up in a pink bow.

"Is it someone's birthday, Eric?"

"I thought this would amuse you."

"I used that once, you know. Ages ago."

This reminded Heidigger of a story, which Dorn listened to. He excused himself to use the bathroom. Unlike the room in Tampa, it had no bidet.

When he had finished, Heidigger wanted to talk about the death of Emil Karnofsky. He said that no one seemed to know how the burglars had gained entrance to the building. Dorn thought this was possible, but not terribly likely.

"For curiosity, Miles, how well did you have your own plan worked out?"

"To the last damned detail," he said bitterly. "It would have been a hell of a lot slicker than what happened."

"You had a way to get inside?"

He nodded. "A psychiatrist. Moritz Greenspan."

"A Jew?"

"No, an Australian Bushfellow. Yes, a Jew. I actually went and stretched out on his couch for fifty intolerable minutes and talked about how depressed I was. The shit wouldn't even take part in the conversation. I paid him fifty dollars and had to do all the talking."

This, predictably, reminded Heidigger of a joke. It was one Dorn had heard.

"I was going to go back again. I made an appointment. The only time it's difficult to get into the building is late at night. At other times you just see any of the doctors there, and you're inside."

"You were going to take Karnofsky out during the day?"

"No, of course not," he said, impatiently. "I was going to see the idiot doctor and then hide somewhere in the building until four in the morning. They watch the entrances and elevators, but they don't check anything else. There were several apartments empty, tenants on vacation. I could have let myself in and had a nap until it was time."

"And you'd do it while Karnofsky and the nigger were both asleep?"

"Of course. I wasn't sure of method. I was thinking of insulin shock. That's easy. Or an air bubble in a vein. He used a needle all the time, one more puncture wouldn't have surprised anybody."

"A damned shame. There are the stupidest rumors. That it was a power play within his union. That the Mafia rubbed him out. Stupid. You know, I couldn't believe it was your work." He laughed shortly. "Fifty dollars, a dollar a minute to tell some silly old Jew your troubles. And the troubles were not even your own!"

On a television set in another hotel room, Dorn watched an excerpt from a press conference called by Governor William Roy Guthrie to explain his declining an invitation to address a convention of New American Patriots in Milwaukee. "I'd certainly like to go up there and talk to those folks," Dorn heard him say. "It does my heart good to see that people up North are beginning to see things the way we all been seeing 'em down here for years. But it's my job to see to the problems of the good people of Louisiana. That's what they pay me for, not to go flying all over the country. Besides, I'm not too sure how safe it'd be up there. I'd have to go and sit out in the sun through a lot of Louisiana summers before I felt secure in that part of the country."

A reporter asked the governor if his decision stemmed from a reluctance to play second fiddle to James Danton Rhodine, already slated as principal speaker.

"You fellows come up with the strangest things," Guthrie said. "I wouldn't mind hearing Rhodine myself. Just because he's seen fit to jump on our southern bandwagon is nothing for me to object to. I'd like to see all the good people in America jump on the bandwagon. There's room for the lot of us."

While in the microfilm room of the New York Public Library, Dorn had read a number of stories that had nothing whatsoever to do with Emil Karnofsky. One of these was a human-interest piece on Willie Jackson.

Willie Jackson was a 63-year-old Baton Rouge shoeshine boy. In his earlier capacity as commissioner of public highways, Guthrie had stopped every morning at Will Jackson's post outside the State Office Building for a shine. Upon election to the governorship in 1962, Guthrie had sent instructions to Jackson to be at his office every morning at nine to shine Guthrie's shoes.

Willie Jackson was not the sort given to voluble complaint. But he seemed to have said something to somebody, and one of the many reporters who despised Guthrie managed to come up with the story. It seemed that Jackson was not at all happy with his new post. The governor's office in the State Capitol Building was a brisk ten-minute walk from his post outside the State Office Building, and after he had arrived, Guthrie frequently kept him waiting for as long as an hour before letting him apply wax to leather. As a result, Willie Jackson was being done out of a major portion of his income. Furthermore, according to the original story, Guthrie never gave him more than a dime.

The *Times* story went on to explain that when Guthrie had read all this he was enraged. As it happened, he was genuinely fond of Jackson and thought he had been doing him a good turn, that his appointment would lend him status with his peers. It had never occured to him that he was costing the man money. Finally, and this was the sorest point of all, he invariably gave Jackson a dollar, which was considerably more than the average payment for a shoeshine in Baton Rouge, Louisiana.

Dorn suspected that Guthrie's first impulse must have been to throw Jackson into a room with a naked white girl and let him die of shock. But the Louisiana governor had style. He immediately shot a bill through the state legislature appointing Willie Jackson official Louisiana Shoeshine Boy for life, and authorizing at taxpayers' expense the erection of a permanent shoeshine stand on the steps of the State Capitol Building.

And every morning, as Governor William Roy Guthrie and his four-man bodyguard walked to the governor's office, Guthrie stopped for a shine. Willie Jackson shined his shoes, and Guthrie gave him a dollar, and virtually every newspaper in America had run, at least once, a photograph of this little ceremony. Some of the photos showed Guthrie standing with his hands on his hips,

80

beaming around a fat cigar. In others he was depicted leaning over to rub Jackson's nappy white head for luck.

Dorn loved the story, and had got to the point where he could not think of Guthrie without thinking of Willie Jackson. Periodically he found himself experiencing the same sort of grudging affection for Guthrie that he did for Eric Heidigger, and he suspected the reasons, whatever they might be, were not all that dissimilar.

On Dorn's second and final trip to Baton Rouge, he took along his copies of the Black Panther newspaper, along with some of the contents of the parcel Heidigger had given him. He brought other supplies as well.

It was not so easy to move around unobtrusively in Baton Rouge as in a city like New York. Dorn devoted a few hours to following Willie Jackson after he had closed his shoeshine stand for the day. It was in his mind to secrete copies of the Black Panther paper in Jackson's room, but the more he considered this the less advantageous it seemed. He ultimately buried the papers in a trash can.

He spent several more hours determining the pattern of surveillance in the Capitol area. The actual process of secreting an explosive charge in the base of the shoeshine stand took less than ten minutes, start to finish.

One item in Heidigger's parcel that Dorn did not take to Baton Rouge was a squat plastic cube the size and shape of a pack of regular cigarettes. There was a button on it, set at a level with the surface of the device. When depressed, it would emit a high-frequency signal that would activate a companion device which was presently in Baton Rouge. One night in Willow Falls, Dorn used a knife blade to pry the device apart at the seams. He made an interesting modification of the device and put it back together again.

He spent the next day with Jocelyn. At one point she told him that he seemed to be in an unusual mood.

"It's true," he admitted. "I am apprehensive."

"Of what?"

"I can't remember the last time I had something to lose. The sensation is enervating."

"Something to lose?"

"You."

"You're silly," she said, kissing him.

He went back to Baltimore. It took him more time than he had anticipated to learn the name and find the apartment. It was late when he knocked on the door. A gaunt black woman with cautious eyes opened it.

He said, "Royal Carter?"

"What you want with him?"

"It's private."

She frowned disapproval but turned and went into another room. A few moments later the boy with the Afro haircut came to the door. He looked at Dorn without recognition.

Dorn tugged at the lobe of his ear, then put his finger to his lips. Royal Carter's eyes narrowed for an instant. Then he nodded shortly.

Dorn said something inane about Methodist missionary activity in Botswana. While he talked, he held a piece of paper so that Carter could read what was written on it. It said: *Greyhound terminal men's room 20 minutes.*

Carter took in the message and nodded curtly. Then when Dorn paused in the middle of his speech about Botswana, he said, "I ain't interested in missions, man," and closed the door in Dorn's face.

A long-distance telephone conversation:

"I'm in Egypt, man."

"No trouble?"

"No. Take forever to grow that hair back, that's all that bothers me."

"It's for a good cause."

"No complaints. Hate having to wait three more days. That's all. But if an old man like him can hold up his end, I can carry mine. The way he stands there and toms, and then to deliver like this."

"I hope you haven't talked to him."

"No, I'm cool. I just watch him is all. And I don't hang around too much."

"Good."

82

"Thursday, then."

"Good."

Dorn did not like the waiting either. Too many things could go wrong and he could not control them. Royal Carter was alone in Baton Rouge with no one on hand to keep his nerve up. The plastic object in Carter's pocket could be activated, through nervousness or accident, at any time. Many times in his career Dorn had had to run an amateur, and he had learned early to stay close enough to the runner to hold onto the reins.

This was not possible. It was very important to him that he not be in Baton Rouge when the shit hit the fan. It was, further, quite necessary that he be with Jocelyn, and this saddled him with the three-day waiting period. She was in New York, enduring a summit meeting with her father.

"He'll play the heavy parent role," she had said. "It's no problem. I can handle him. I'll be back by Wednesday at the latest. Will you miss me?"

"Perhaps a little."

"And what will you do while I'm gone?"

"Rest," he said. "And conserve my strength."

He wanted her to be with him when it happened. It did not seem likely to him that she would make an association between his absences from Willow Falls and the violent deaths of prominent persons. He was gone frequently when nothing happened, and there were all too many violent deaths, unconnected with Dorn, that took place while they were together.

He occasionally wondered if she was having an adverse effect on his judgment. He knew that, but for her, there would be no need for this hectic running back and forth between Willow Falls and other parts of the country. He had to preserve this cover of his only because his relationship with her was a part of it. Otherwise he would simply have floated around, constantly mobile, like Heidigger with his Holiday Inns.

He decided that speculation was pointless. But for her, after all, everything would be completely different.

"That rotten fascist bastard. Oh, I hope somebody gets him. I'm not that nonviolent· I think it would be worth dying, to get someone like Guthrie first."

Q.E.D.

On Thursday morning, while Miles Dorn and Jocelyn Perry were weighing the desirability of breakfast against that of remaining in bed a little longer, Royal Carter was drinking coffee at a lunch counter across the street from the State Capitol Building in Baton Rouge, Louisiana. He was so seated on his stool that without moving his head he could glance either out through the window to the Capitol steps or across the counter to the large flyspecked mirror. His eyes would dart first to the right and then to the left. When he looked at his reflection in the mirror, he had to repress the impulse to reach for his head and touch his hair, now uniformly cropped to within a quarter-inch of his scalp. When he looked out the window, his right hand, kept at all times in a pocket of his overalls, automatically fingered a plastic gadget the size and shape of a pack of cigarettes.

He rarely glanced at the clock. He kept wanting to, but didn't. And when a glance out the window for the first time that morning brought him the sight of Governor Guthrie, he did not react in any visible way. Perhaps his heart speeded up, perhaps his blood pressure increased, but he gave no outward sign of excitement.

He remained cool throughout the ritual shining of the shoes, his eyes now fastened upon the ceremony, with no time off for anxious inspections of his mirror image. His right index finger located the button and caressed it with something akin to love.

Dorn had told him how it would happen. How Willie Jackson, the hair nearly rubbed from his head by all those years of racist patronage, would be affixing miniature explosive devices to the undersides of Guthrie's insteps. How Jackson, who could not risk detonating the devices himself, would then remain in his stand, waiting. And how he, Royal Carter, would rid the world of an arch-pig without ever attaching the slightest suspicion to himself.

The shoeshine went on unendurably. It took all his effort to refrain from pushing the button now and getting it over with. Why chance Guthrie's noticing that he had something stuck to his shoes? Why not do it now, and let Willie Jackson go out with him in a blaze of glory?

No, he couldn't do that. Brother Jackson had paid his dues, year after year of dues, year after year of tomming his way through Hell. He had a right not only to live but also to enjoy this moment.

And so he waited, just as Dorn had told him to wait. Waited for the final bit of spit and polish, waited for the snapping of the buffing rag, waited for the rubbing of the white-thatched head, the good-luck rub.

See how good your luck is, Billy Roy!

(*"The essential strategy is to minimize the possibilities of failure. Let him go just so far but no farther. The top of the first deck of steps. Not sooner, or Jackson would be in danger. No farther, however, because every step increases the likelihood of his noticing the plastic on his soles."*)

The cloth snapped, the head was rubbed, the dollar bill passed with a flourish. And Guthrie, flanked by his bodyguard (who, if they survived, would shortly find themselves without a body to guard) turned and mounted the Capitol steps.

One, two, three, four, five . . . .

When Guthrie put his foot upon the top step on the first deck, two things happened in a single thunderclap.

The permanently installed stand of the official Louisiana Shoeshine Boy disappeared.

So did a large portion of the lunch counter diagonally across the street.

"I'm sorry," Jocelyn said. "I don't feel sorry for him."

"Nor do I."

"I mean, I think it's horrible for anyone to have his legs blown off. One at the knee and one at the hip. I get a little sick thinking about it. I flash on it and I look down at my own legs—"

"A horrible thing."

"But if anything, I'm sorry he didn't die. That poor old Uncle Tom, that's the man I feel sorry for. And the people in the luncheonette. Not Guthrie and his pig bodyguard."

Dorn took her hand. "That's not the point," he said. "You don't get rid of racism by getting rid of Guthrie."

"Maybe not, but you have one less racist. And one less loud voice on the subject."

"And you also convince more and more of the uncommitted people that blacks are dangerous and extreme blacks are extremely dangerous. You tell all of the Willie Jacksons in America that they have more to fear from their own kinsmen than from racists like Guthrie. After all, consider this—Guthrie, whatever his attitude, gave Willie Jackson a dollar. What did the bomber give him? Death."

"Then what is a person supposed to do, Miles?"

"Survive."

"Is that all?"

"At times it's chore enough in itself."

" 'Don't do anything because it might make the other side stronger.' Is that what it comes down to?"

"A way to put it."

Her eyes challenged him. "Is that what you learned in your years in Europe? I know you were involved in politics there. Is that the lesson you learned?"

"Part of it."

She nibbled her lip. "I forget who said it, but there's a saying. 'All that is required for the triumph of evil is for good men to do nothing.' "

"I know the saying."

"But you don't care for it?"

"But I do. There is a variation of it, though, that I think is at least as valuable."

"What?"

" 'All that is required for the triumph of evil is for good men to do something wrong.' "

She thought it over. "Who said that?"

"I don't remember."

A newspaper item:

"Governor James Danton Rhodine of Indiana today visited the sickbed of Louisiana's Governor William Roy Guthrie, in good condition after surgery. Rhodine told reporters outside the hospital that he found Guthrie in good spirits and more determined than ever to resume the fight against 'the forces of decadence, subversion, and black despair.' Rhodine called on all Americans of good will to 'take up the torch that lies fallen in Louisiana and spread its light across the nation.' A spokesman for the Indiana governor later denied that there was any racist connotation in the phrase 'black despair.' "

Another newspaper item:

"In a move which informed sources consider linked to the

Guthrie bombing, Prime Minister H. J. Gaansevoort of the Republic of South Africa today canceled a proposed state visit to Washington. The visit, originally scheduled for the second week in August, had drawn heavy fire from black spokesmen; it had been initiated through the office of Vice-President Henry M. Theodore, apparently without direct presidential approval. The White House declined comment . . . . "

A long-distance telephone conversation:
"My profound apologies."
"I had been about to offer congratulations."
"The trouble with untrained help."
"Or mechanical failure."
"Unlikely. The delivery was a day late in the first place. The delivery vessel froze at the switch."
"Repeat."
"Weakness of resolve led to a one-day postponement. There was an excuse, but I think it was a cover."
"Understood."
"Then another freeze, I would suppose, and an attempt at courageous recovery. But by then the ship had almost cleared the horizon."
"Not quite, though."
"No. Annoying. Again, my apologies. I will follow through on this when conditions permit."
"No need."
"Established?"
"Absolutely. A hit is as good as a bull's-eye."
"The voice remains."
"But disembodied."
"True, but commanding allegiance—"
A chuckle. "In no gripping way. The total effect has not been officially told."
"Oh?"
"A low blow indeed. The flock might go clucking after a wingless rooster, but not after a capon."
"Repeat?"
"Say that the count stands at one strike, no balls."
"Understood. Amusing."
"Definitely amusing. Good luck on Case Four."
"Thank you."

ELEVEN

As the summer wore on, one hot day after another, it became gradually evident to Dorn that he was not going to assassinate the mayor of Detroit. He traveled to that city twice, going there with no clear purpose in mind and doing nothing in particular in the time he spent there. He never got a glimpse of Walter Isaac James, although he frequently read his words and saw his features in Detroit newspapers.

It was shaping up as a quiet summer in Detroit. The clash between peace demonstrators and auto workers had not been repeated, and the consequent conflict between the Detroit police and their mayor had been quietly and undramatically resolved. There was a slight stir when Mayor James's office refused application for a permit for an outdoor rally to the New American Patriots. Governor Rhodine of Indiana had been scheduled to address the rally, and the mayor's office delayed processing the permit application on various technical grounds. A move to hold the rally without a permit was quashed by Rhodine himself.

During his second trip to Detroit, Dorn clipped a newsphoto of Walter Isaac James and put it in his pocket. He fell into the habit of carrying it on his person at all times, transferring it from one pair of pants to another along with his wallet and his keys. From time to time, when he was alone in his house in Willow Falls, or while he rode a bus from someplace to someplace else, he would take the scrap of paper from his pocket and gaze for long periods of time into that black ovoid face, as if there were some special message in those features that long contemplation would permit him to divine.

The face was a difficult one for him to read. Time after time he would look at it, an arrangement of black dots on white paper, and all he would see was its color. He wondered at the immense implications of blackness.

He had read once that black ants and red ants were implacable enemies. Whenever a black ant and a red ant met, they fought until one or the other was dead. He wondered if this was true, and he thought of taking a book from the library on insect life, but never got around to it.

There came a point, after he had taken that scrap of paper from his pocket an incalculable number of times, when at last he began to see the face before the color. This might have happened sooner had James possessed any dominant features, a beak of a nose or piercing eyes or oddly-shaped ears, but the bland regularity of his features delayed the process. There was nothing about that face that caught the eyes, nothing specific that left a bookmark in the memory. But finally he came to look at the photo and see the man.

Perhaps he had begun to realize even before then that he did not intend to terminate Case Four. It later seemed to him that this was so. Once he passed the veneer of blackness, once the face of Walter Isaac James spoke directly to him, the decision was inescapable.

But how? How to let this man live? Another bungled attempt would not go down well. He could make his little trips, to Detroit or elsewhere. He could give the painstaking appearance of preparation. But for how long?

He could not procrastinate forever. Sooner or later push would come to shove. Sooner or later the Rubicon would be reached, and either crossed or not.

And so he went on taking the photograph from his pocket and looking at that quiet face, those open eyes. He would look at the man and try to think of ways not to kill him, and then he would sigh and return the scrap of paper to his pocket.

In Birmingham, Vice-President Henry M. Theodore told a chamber of commerce luncheon that disorder and anarchy were the greatest threats to the free enterprise system in the entire history of the American nation. "There can be no compromise with these divisive forces," he said. "Since the days when pioneers carved a nation out of a wilderness, the American businessman has been history's architect and builder. At this critical point in our history, he cannot sit idly by and watch his proudest structure torn stone from stone, brick from brick, sacked one room at a time by barbarians." The vice-president's talk was several times interrupted by spontaneous applause, and he received a standing ovation at its conclusion. Outside, black and white protesters attempting to picket his appearance were routed by a mob of angry whites. Assertions of police brutality were widespread.

At the Los Angeles Coliseum, James Danton Rhodine spoke to a crowd of New American Patriots. Among other things, he accused the administration of deliberately prolonging the Asian war. "An unholy alliance of Wall Street money power has shackled the mightiest military machine in the history of the world," he charged. "The Shylocks and Fagins of New York work hand in evil hand with the heirs of Lenin and Trotsky and Marx. With the aid of that speckled band of traitors, they spill the blood of God-fearing American youths in a war that could otherwise be won overnight." When a crowd of anti-war protesters attempted to enter the hall, Rhodine's contingent of marshals instantly surround them, beat them into submission, and turned them out into the street. The marshals, uniformly tall, well-built, short-haired and neatly groomed, were becoming a standard fixture at NAP rallies. They dressed alike in tight khaki pants and royal blue shirts. Their brisk and efficient treatment of the Los Angeles protesters was jubilantly applauded by the crowd, and Rhodine himself praised them as representing the highest virtues of the youth of America. "Look at them," he exhorted his hearers. "They are not long-haired or unkempt or wild-eyed. They are the sort of young men who made America great. They are the young men who will make America great once again."

Jocelyn had a dual effect upon the waiting, the stalling. Her presence made indolence bearable. She lent focus to his life and made a place for his mind to go when he did not want to think of Walter Isaac James. He had discovered within himself a capacity to lose himself almost completely in her arms. His coming in the precious envelope of her flesh was the little death that the French called it. There was each time that perfect instant when, by becoming, he ceased to be.

And yet her role in his life added too a lazy urgency, oddly enervating. Because she existed, because of the part she played, his own need to resolve the situation was so much the greater.

Heidigger had said that James was to be killed in hot weather. Detroit lay hot under the July sun, hotter still in August. The city maintained an uneasy calm. Policemen muttered to themselves but kept a light rein in black neighborhoods. Polish machinists in Hamtramck cursed the black mayor and thanked God for the autonomy that made their enclave a suburban island inside the Detroit sea. The lid might be shaky but the lid remained on, and Dorn looked at a black man's photograph and sought a way to keep the lid in place.

He considered near-misses. He thought of running a gunman and tipping the runner to the police at the last second. He thought of putting a bullet in an arm or leg, canonizing James with partial martyrdom. But even a close attempt on the mayor might spark a black riot, while anything less than success would go down badly with Heidigger.

Often he awoke with the conviction that he had dreamed of James and the nagging suspicion that his dream had held an answer. But he could never remember these dreams.

One afternoon, elaborately casual, she said, "There's a sort of party tonight. Not too many people. About a dozen kids or so."

He kept his feelings off his face, out of his voice. "You ought to go," he said. "You can't spend all your time with an old man."

"You're not an old man. I think you just say that so I'll tell you you're not."

"Oh? How old is your father?"

"Oh, come on, Miles."

"You once told me. Fifty? I am fifty-four."

"You've never met my father."

But he had, once, although of course he had not told her. Once in New York, between sieges at the microfilm viewer, he had walked a few blocks to the firm that manufactured beads for dressmakers. On some pretext he got himself shown into the man's office, then let it develop that it was another Howard Perry he was looking for. Jocelyn's father was sleek, balding, with pouches under his eyes and a bitter look about the mouth. It had pleased Dorn, later, to examine his own reflection in a mirror and to remark that he looked younger and more fit than Perry.

"You think I should go?"

"But certainly."

"They invited both of us, Miles. What's the matter—did you think we were a secret?"

"I hadn't thought about it."

"Well, my friends know that you and I are a thing."

"A thing?"

"Lovers."

He realized that it had not even occurred to him to wonder whether her friends knew this. When she was with him it was as if she ceased to exist apart from him. No, he corrected himself, it was more that what they shared, what they were to each other, had no points of reference to the rest of the world.

"I thought maybe you'd like to go."

"Why don't you go without me? I would be out of place, don't you think?"

"Well, it's a couples thing," she said, not pressing. "I wouldn't go alone, that wouldn't be cool. But it's not important."

"You would like me to go with you?"

"Only, you know, if you want."

"Why not?"

There were six couples at the downtown apartment when he and Jocelyn arrived. Two more students came ten minutes later. Dorn smiled through introductions but made no attempt to remember names. He sat cross-legged on a cushion on the floor and accepted a glass of too-sweet wine. He listened in on various conversations, ranging in topic from politics to music. His eyes wandered around the large, sparsely-furnished room. Several posters caught his eye. One was a list of instructions on proper behavior in the event of a nuclear attack. It told the reader to curl himself up in a ball and place his head down between his legs. *"Now kiss your ass good-bye,"* it concluded. Another showed a Nazi flag, a black swastika stark on a red field. Above it, English words were written in German Gothic type: *"It's your flag; love it or leave it."*

He finished his wine and began to circulate around the room, moving from one knot of people to another, joining passively but easily in a variety of conversations. He observed the boys and girls with interest, not attempting to distinguish one individual from another but wanting merely to develop a collective impression of them. Surface aspects—beards, long hair, dress—clouded his view at first. Like James's blackness, he thought. But familiarity taught one to see past the surface, to gaze through it.

He turned once to find Jocelyn at his elbow. "Having a good time?"

"Yes. I'm enjoying myself."

"Are you? I was afraid you wouldn't. But I wanted you to meet my friends."

He was refilling his wineglass when a voice said, "Mr. Dorn?" He turned to look at one of the boys, taller than he, clean-shaven, hair to his shoulders. The boy had an arm around a very short girl. Nevertheless, Dorn knew instantly that this boy had slept with Jocelyn.

"Miles," he corrected, smiling gently. "I'd sooner feel no more ancient than I absolutely must."

"Jocelyn tells me you're opposed to revolutionary violence."

"That's true."

"I suppose you take the position that violence never solved anything."

"Not at all. It's often a solution. Sometimes a final solution, as someone once called it."

"Then you oppose it for humanitarian reasons?"

The patronizing assurance of the young. "That is reason enough, wouldn't you say? But it is also beside the point. You needn't tell me about omelets and broken eggs. I might agree with you, I might not. I oppose violence because of its effects."

"Which are?"

"Violence in return. Action equals reaction, a law of physics. Except that in politics the reaction is often greater than the action. Rocks bring bullets."

"So you believe that confrontations have to stay peaceful. That's a good theory, but how do you explain it to Jon Yerkes when a pig's bullet takes his hand off? Or what do you say to the Panthers when the cops come through the door with their guns blasting away? Don't shoot back? Just stand there and get killed?"

The boy had raised his voice, and others were beginning to circle around, hanging on the dialogue. There was a subtle manhood test here, Dorn decided. The boy talked of politics, but it was their mutual relationship with Jocelyn that was the conversation's raison d'être. Dorn's impulse was to give ground.

Instead, he said, "You misunderstand me. You make a greater

93

distinction than I between violent and nonviolent political action. I think either is a mistake."

"Oh, man, I don't buy that. Take a look around you. This country is on the way to a revolution."

"So it seems."

"And it damn well needs one. You can't reform the system. It's gone beyond that point." He went into an indictment of the country's ills, making no points that had not occurred to Dorn and few with which he was inclined to disagree. He paused for breath, then looked down at Dorn again, setting his jaw. "The revolution's coming," he said. "Everything we do makes it come just that much faster."

"Absolutely."

"Even the acts that bring reaction. Every time a student is clubbed or bayoneted or shot, ten more students stop being liberals and turn into radicals. Every time the other side makes a move, our side grows stronger."

"I agree."

"Then you've lost me, man. If you've got a point, I don't know where you're hiding it."

Dorn put down his wineglass. "Everything you do provokes a reaction," he said carefully, "and every reaction strengthens the left. I think that this is beyond dispute. Every day the left grows and every day the right grows. There is a line of Yeats. '*Things fall apart. The center cannot hold*.' This happens, it is happening now, even as we talk. Every day more people take a side, one side or the other. Every day more people find a centrist position untenable."

"That's *my* point."

"And mine," Dorn said, softly, smiling, "mine is that as soon as you succeed in forcing matters to a crisis, you guarantee that you lose. Because there are more of them than there are of you. Many more of them. Every day brings the left closer to its maximum strength of perhaps twenty-five percent of the population. Every day brings the right closer to a maximum of perhaps seventy-five percent of the population."

"I don't know where you get your figures—"

"Out of the air. But I would be surprised if the gulf is not even wider than I've postulated it."

"We have the blacks, we have the students, we have more and more of the liberals, we have the poor whites—"

"The poor whites? I think not."

"But we will. Sooner or later the poor whites and the white working class are going to see where their best interests lie."

"Precisely."

"Huh?"

"Their interests lie in keeping blacks in a subservient position. I do not find it remarkable that they have already figured this out. What I find remarkable is that anyone seriously expects them to decide otherwise."

They argued this point. Dorn yielded with smiles and soft words. The discussion slowed.

"Anyway," the boy said, "I don't see the point of talking in terms of numbers. I don't buy your numbers, but I think they're irrelevant. The revolution isn't going to come about through an election. Maybe democracy is outmoded to begin with. You can't call this fucking country a democracy."

"Nonsense."

"Man, when you look what's going down—"

"Every stable government in the history of the world has been a democracy."

The boy's hands turned to fists. He said, "I think that's the most outrageous statement I've ever heard."

"That's because you haven't heard the rest of it. Every stable government has been a democracy in that it has ruled with the implicit support of the majority of its population. The form of government has been immaterial. Feudalism, monarchy, parliamentary system, fascist or communist dictatorship."

"Then by your standards Nazi Germany was a democracy."

"And by yours as well," Dorn said mildly. "Hitler won an election, you know."

Back at his house she said, "I should have warned you about Jerry. But you sort of made an idiot out of him, didn't you?"

"Not really. And he's not an idiot. But when people tell each other the same things over a long period of time, they become unused to questioning their beliefs. I see things from a different perspective, and one he couldn't easily categorize."

"I wonder how much you meant of what you said."

"Do you? All of it."

"But then—"

"Yes?"

"Then what do we do? What is the right thing for people in our position to do?"

"Survive."

"Just survive?"

"Survive. Stay out of politics, stay out of jail. Stay alive."

Her face was troubled. "Now I sound like Jerry, but Christ, Miles, you grew up in Europe, you saw your own country over-run by Nazis. Is that what you would have told a Jew in Germany? Survive?"

"It is what I would have told anyone in Germany, Jew or not. At one time I would have advised strengthening the Weimar Republic so that Hitler could not occur. After that I would have said, 'Go, leave the country.'"

"Survive."

"Yes."

"I don't know if I've got all of this together. We should stop fighting. We should just survive. We should shave and cut our hair and get straight jobs and look like everybody else. Is that it?"

He reached out a hand, stroked her hair. "Don't cut your hair," he said, smiling. "And please don't shave."

"I'm serious."

"Then I shall be serious. No, that is not what I think. I think you are very special, you young people. I think your life-style is very special. I think you should go on growing your hair and your beards and finding yourselves in communes and listening to your music. Read. Think. Grow. Discover. And wait."

"For what?"

"For more of you to be born. For more of them to die. The future does belong to you, you know. If you don't try to make it come too soon."

"'All things come to him who waits.'"

"They do. Not as soon as he may wish. But they do."

Do they, Jocelyn? Or am I an old man making new mistakes? Presumptuous of me. Presumptuous of an assassin to warn against the fruits of violence. Of a terrorist to counsel patience.

Perhaps it is too late. The tide swings their way, and perhaps it cannot be stopped. Perhaps one ought not to go gently. Perhaps one ought to die on one's feet. Better far, I am told, than to live on one's knees.

But I am not altogether certain I believe that, Jocelyn.

I like your friends, Jocelyn. I like the beauty of their open faces. I like their warmth. I like their easy humor and their ancient seriousness. I argued with one of them out of male foolishness, but I liked them all. And they seemed to like me.

What would they think of me, I wonder, if they knew? And you, Jocelyn? If you knew?

Until a morning late in August when she slipped out of the house after breakfast, leaving him at the kitchen table with a cup of tea. Off to buy some groceries, off to feed her cat. He looked out the window at the robins' nest, empty now. Vertigo might as well live with them, he thought. She already kept things at the house. Some of her clothes were in his closet, some of her books on his shelves. Her radio was perched on his kitchen table. And yet, although she slept almost every night in his bed, she still had a room that was, in part, home to her. He wondered if he ought to say anything about the cat, or if that would center her life excessively upon him.

The robins again. The more you loved them, the more you had to prepare them for flight. For life apart from you. And the more it tore you to do so.

Something made him switch on the radio. Music, a song she liked and he did not, came as an unwelcome reminder of the gulf between them. He reached to change the station, but the record ended and a newscast came on.

And so he heard, sitting there alone, sitting in his kitchen with her radio playing. He heard that racial warfare still raged openly in the streets of Detroit, with no sign of abatement, after an ambush the night before in which gunfire had claimed the lives of Mayor Walter Isaac James, his wife, and two of their five children.

He put his head on the table and wept.

He held the photo in his hands and stared at the blackness, past the blackness, deep into the face.

Walter Isaac James. First-term mayor of Detroit. Black. Economic and social moderate. Foreign policy views unstated. Enjoys near-total support of black constituency plus strong support of white power structure, professionals, intellectuals. Relationship improving with white working class. Efficient administrator . . . .

I tried, Mr. James. I said, this man shall live. This man's life is worthwhile, he shall live. And so I waited, and stalled, and created the appearance of preparation. And a pair of beer-drinking ex-marines decided that the crippling of William Roy Guthrie could not go unavenged.

. . . . Termination ideally to be as dramatic as possible. Perhaps family could be included . . . .

Oh, it was dramatic, Mr. James. The mayoral limousine caught in cross fire. And part of your family indeed included. A wife. Two children. And the people burning the city down and killing one another.

Forgive me, Mr. James. For shirking my duty.

A long-distance telephone conversation:

"Congratulations. You have outdone yourself. The results exceed all expectations."

"Thank you."

"What about your tools, though? They've been picked up. I hope you cleaned them before you put them away."

"Completely."

"You're quite certain? Those vessels will leak under pressure, you know."

"A vessel cannot spill what it does not contain."

"Such ships could be sunk, if you wanted. As a sort of insurance policy."

"No need."

"As you prefer. There was some concern, incidentally, over the time factor."

"The arrangements demanded careful handling."

"So I suggested to the critical voices. And my judgment was vindicated, for which my own thanks, by the way. Everyone is more than pleased."

"I'm gratified."

"Good! Oh, you can forget Case Five, if you wish. It's been officially downgraded in importance."

"I've already begun."

"Let it go, if there's the slightest risk."

"No risk at all. And I'd rather clean the slate."

"Perfectionist."

"Let us merely say craftsman."

"As you will."

TWELVE

The policeman said,

"I'm trying to think, a drugstore at this hour. There's an all-night place near the Thirtieth Street station. You have a car?"

"No, I flew in just a few hours ago."

"Because it's a long walk, and you might have a time getting a cab."

"I thought they would have aspirin at the hotel desk."

"If it's just an aspirin, there's a White Tower three, four blocks down on Market. It's just a coffee place but they generally have a bottle of aspirin around."

"We have White Towers in Indianapolis," Dorn said.

"That where you're from? That's Rhodine's state, isn't it?"

"Yes."

"I guess he's a cinch for reelection."

"He's very popular."

"He's getting to be pretty popular here in Philadelphia, too. A lot of people are starting to listen to what he has to say."

"Your own mayor is popular, isn't he?"

"What, O'Dowd?" The policeman frowned. "My position, I'm not supposed to have anything to say about the mayor."

"It's a free country."

"A lot freer these days if you don't happen to be a cop." He swung his nightstick absently against the palm of his hand. "Put it this way, if they held an election tomorrow O'Dowd wouldn't stand a chance."

"Is that so?"

"He's popular with a certain element. Why the hell not, he wants to give them the whole city on a platter. I shouldn't be talking like this."

"I'm from out of town."

"Yeah, and it's a free country. Freedom of speech, unless you happen to work hard and pay your taxes and try to live decent. Then they expect you to keep your mouth shut. My old man was on the force. Also an uncle, one of my mother's brothers—as a matter of fact he's still on the force. I grew up taking it for granted that I would be a cop. I never even thought of being anything else. If I knew it was gonna be like this."

"It must be very difficult."

"You wouldn't believe it." He looked at Dorn. "At least where you're from they let law enforcement people do their job. They don't handcuff them. I'll give you an example. We had a situation here the other day that didn't even make the papers, but to give you an idea. This buck over in the center city had himself a skinful and decided to stick a knife in his wife. Whether she was actually his wife or not I couldn't say. Anyway, he takes a knife this long and sticks it in her. Lucky he doesn't kill her. So naturally somebody calls us, and they send a car around and rush her to the hospital and take him downtown.

"Now this is no civil rights thing, is it? I mean it's a case of a man cutting up a woman. ADW, assault with a deadly weapon, maybe attempted second-degree homicide if the district attorney has a hair up, which he usually doesn't. But nine times out of ten it's nothing at all because the wife decides she loves him and says she fell on the knife, or she stabbed herself, or whatever the hell she says, and the charges are dropped. But it's no civil rights thing, it's no police brutality.

"Listen to this. They surround the police car. Dozens of people. They start rocking it, they won't let 'em take this drunk downtown. So one of the guys in the car calls downtown and explains the situation. 'Let him go,' the order comes back. 'But he's drunk and he wants to kill people.' 'It doesn't matter, let him go.'

"So they let him go. And the crowd lets the cops go, and they drive away. But that's not enough for these people. They go nuts, the rocks start flying, the store windows go. Black, white, it doesn't matter who owns these businesses. It's a hot night and

100

this is an easy way to pick up a free television set and a few quarts of Scotch. So everybody starts looting.

"And we do nothing because our hands are tied. 'Let 'em loot. Let 'em cool down by theirselves.' So in a couple hours they have all the liquor and clothes and television sets they want and they go home, and there's no big story for the papers, and all over the country people look at Philly and say 'O'Dowd knows how to keep things cool.' All he keeps cool is the police force. Jesus, I shouldn't be mouthing off like this, but I didn't get on the force to sit around watching people burn down the country."

"It's frightening," Dorn said.

"It really is. You want a cigarette?"

"I don't smoke."

"Yeah, I been trying to quit myself, but it's impossible. I don't know. When I was a kid it wasn't just me, with my father and all, but everybody respected the cops. He was this tall guy in a uniform who helped people. You know something? You take your average criminal, I mean a hardened professional criminal, and he respects the police. He knows we have a job and we have to do it. But these people nowadays, to them we're pigs for doing our job. For trying to keep the city together. They say the job isn't worth doing. These people, when a building is burning they stand and throw rocks at firemen. Guys trying to put out a fire and save a building, and these people stand and throw rocks at them."

"You would think there must be an answer."

"But where the hell is it? There's a lot of guys leaving the force. Going out in the suburbs where they don't have to contend with this, where they can still do the job they're being paid to do. Others leaving police work altogether. The pay you get is nothing when you look at the dangers and the abuse you have to put up with. But I believe in this job, you know? Somebody has to do it. What happens if everybody throws his hands up and says the hell with it?"

"Then you have anarchy," Dorn said.

"Yeah. Anarchy. I guess it's a lot different where you're from. Another world, it must be."

"Completely different."

"I voted for the President in the last election. You know who a lot of cops voted for? What's-his-name, that had his legs blown off. Guthrie."

"Oh, yes."

"But I couldn't see it myself. I mean what would he really know about running the country? About foreign policy? So I voted for the President, but if they had an election tomorrow I don't know what I'd do. You know who they're talking about more and more? Well, you would know, being from his state. Your man Rhodine."

"Yes, he's building up quite a following."

"To tell you the truth, he's a little far-out for my tastes. There's a lot of talk that he's coming down pretty hard on the Jews. Reading between the lines. I don't know about that. But Jesus, we need somebody to take a strong stand on what's happening in this country. It's not getting better. Maybe this country needs a man like Rhodine to get things moving in the right direction again."

"He knows how to maintain law and order."

"Yeah. And we could use some of that. You know who else I like is Theodore. Of course he hasn't got Rhodine's style. But I like what he's got to say."

On the flight North he had sat with eyes closed and hands in lap. The newsphoto of Walter Isaac James was in his pocket. Still.

Jocelyn, I made a mistake and Detroit is burning. Something —your love, a black man's face—blurred my vision. I no longer saw myself plain.

I am a killer, Jocelyn. Whatever shoes I wear, I cannot walk other than on an assassin's feet. I committed the great error of forgetting this central fact. I, a gun in another man's hand, presumed to be a hand myself.

From now on, Jocelyn, I shall remember who I am.

They had aspirin at the White Tower. Dorn, who would have asked for some anyway out of a regard for detail, had a headache by the time he reached the coffee shop. He found this amusing. He took two aspirin tablets and drank a glass of iced tea. Twice he found himself reaching for the clipping in his pocket. Both times he caught himself and shook his head, annoyed.

He walked back to his hotel. He passed several uniformed policemen in the few blocks but did not see the one with whom he had spoken. He picked up his key at the desk and went to his room. Inside, he locked the door and affixed the chain bolt. The *Do Not Disturb* sign was in place upon the doorknob.

Patrick John O'Dowd. Second-term mayor of Philadelphia. Liberal Republican. National aspirations. Charismatic. Social radical, economic conservative. National appeal to youthful left-centrists. Strong secondary black appeal. Focal point of white working-class hatred throughout eastern seaboard. Termination recommended but not urgent. Natural or accidental termination advised. Age: 47. Married . . .

He took the photograph of the dead mayor of Detroit from his pocket. He set it on the bed and sat on the edge of the bed and looked down at the photograph.

He heard Eric Heidigger's voice echoing:

(". . . the alternative, Miles Dorn. The mistake everyone makes is to believe that the alternative to change is preservation of the status quo. And this is so rarely true. The alternative to change is another sort of change. You know this.")

"I betrayed you," he told James. "By seeking to preserve you, I in fact betrayed you. For I could have given you so much better a death. At my hands you would have died peacefully and quietly and safely. I would have left not three but five of your children to honor your memory, and their mother would have lived to care for them."

He got to his feet. It would be good to sleep a few hours in this narrow bed. It would be wise to devote a day or two to reconnaissance and planning. But he felt an urgency that could not be denied.

He placed the photograph of Walter Isaac James in an ashtray on top of the dresser. He struck a match. "Forgive me," he said aloud. The photo flared and burned, and he watched even as he wondered at his own unaccustomed participation in the ceremony.

He flushed the ashes down the toilet. Then he opened his window and let himself out onto the fire escape, closing the window after him to within a few inches of the sill. He climbed down five flights, then let himself drop the last flight to the pavement below. He landed lightly, on the balls of his feet, and waited long enough to assure himself that his departure had attracted no attention.

Margaret Keller O'Dowd professed herself incapable of believing the fact of her husband's suicide. "He was too much involved with life. He loved challenges, he loved to test himself in difficult situations. Of course he was under stress, but there was something in Pat that responded to stress. Sometimes he was depressed. He was one man in an impossible job at an impossible time. Of course he would get depressed. But he knew how to triumph over depression. And he was a Catholic, he was always close to the Church. How could he possibly kill himself?"

And yet it was impossible that he had not. The facts were clear enough. Shortly after midnight he had said good-night to his wife and stayed up in his study, going over reports of the latest school board crisis. The school situation had weighed heavily on his mind of late and seemed to be insoluble. When one crisis was resolved another sprang up in its place. He sat at his desk and smoked heavily and initialed reports.

By morning he had still not come to bed. The door to his study was locked from the inside. Attempts to arouse him from without failed. One of the policemen posted outside the mayoral residence was summoned. He kicked the door in and found O'Dowd hanging from a ceiling beam. He had used a cord from the study's drapes to hang himself. He had cut the cord with a paper knife, and shreds of fiber adhered to its blade. He had stood on his desk chair, then kicked the chair over.

No one could have been in the room with him. There were no signs of another presence, no signs of a struggle, no signs that anything other than simple suicide had taken place.

Nor had there been a note. Press reports managed to suggest in an oblique fashion that such a note might have been repressed, either by the authorities or by the mayor's widow. Close associates of O'Dowd's testified to his increasing periods of depression and frustration over the political situation in Philadelphia and throughout the nation. His deepening sorrow over the continuance of the Indo-China War was also mentioned.

In Willow Falls, Dorn several times looked with longing at the cord of his venetian blinds. He read Blake and Yeats and Auden and Arnold.

"Oh love, let us be true to one another . . . ." He did not kill himself, or leave the country.

THIRTEEN

But if he could not leave the country, he could yet send himself out of reach of time and space, and if true death eluded him, he could taste *la petite mort* over and over again.

His appetite for her did not diminish. If anything it increased, and his capacity remained its equal. This astonished Dorn. Sexual pleasure had never played a strong role in his life, and in recent years he had thought himself to have outgrown it. Now it seemed he could hardly have been farther from the truth.

He occasionally wondered how his life might have turned out if he had ever loved anyone in the past.

For as long as he possibly could, he spent all his time in Willow Falls and as much of it as possible in her company. There were short trips, any number of them, that he might profitably have made. He did not make them. There was research he could usefully have undertaken. He did not undertake it. In all too short a time, he knew, he would have to devote himself to Case Six, the final and most important phase of the entire operation. When that time came, it would demand his complete attention. Until then, until the very last minute, he intended to give his complete attention to Jocelyn.

And so, although he duly read the papers and listened to the newscasts, nothing that he heard weighed very heavily upon him. Speeches, whether by Theodore or Rhodine or the President, did not much affect him. The periodic reports of riots and shootings and confrontations and demonstrations came to his attention but did not hold it long. He knew what was likely to happen and was neither surprised nor gratified when such things came to pass.

One day he saw a patch of overhead sky darken at the passage of a huge flock of small birds. Migrants from Canada bound for a winter in Argentina. The local birds had not yet begun gathering themselves for flight. But soon, he thought. Too soon.

There was a night when their lovemaking reached an almost painful peak. His climax fooled him—he truly thought himself to be dying, not *petite mort* but *grande mort*. Afterward he lay listening to his heart and considering the perfection of such a death.

But then he saw the tableau from without, not merely the pure personal pleasure of so dying but the horror of it for her, to emerge from the languor of love and discover that one held a dead man in one's arms. The image jolted him, and brought with it the unwelcome realization that he had postponed their parting too long. This sweet death was an indulgence of self. She had to go on living, and the longer they were thus together the more difficult her situation would be.

He felt tears behind his eyes, and breathed deeply, and willed them away.

Then she said, "Miles? The fall term started last week. I didn't enroll."

"I thought you were going to."

"I was. I went through all the shit of getting reaccepted, and then I just couldn't hack the whole business. I figured I would just drop out again sooner or later and I couldn't do that to everybody, go back just to drop out again."

"What are you going to do?"

"I don't know."

"Have you spoken to your parents?"

"They want me to come home. But that's out. No way." She ran a hand down his chest, gripped him gently for a moment. "Some of the kids are talking about this commune in North Carolina. Up in the hills around Asheville."

"And you were thinking of going?"

"I was thinking you might like to go for a couple of weeks. It's supposed to be an interesting life-style. They grow their own food and make all their own belongings. The idea is to become as self-sufficient as possible and to live naturally, without doing badness to the ecology. Recycling wastes and living in balance with nature. That trip."

"It does sound interesting."

"A lot of the communes are into drugs in a heavy way. Or else they turn into cults. There's a leader, and everybody decides he's getting messages from God, and they have to clear it with him before they pick their toes. But the Land People are supposed to be pretty straight."

"Is that what they call themselves? The Land People?"

"Uh-huh. I wondered, you know, if you'd like to see what it's like."

Somewhere inside him something flared and died, like a star going into nova. If only he could shed these feet of his. If only he could be the person who could take this perfect girl to that perfect society.

But that's out. No way.

"I wish I could do this," he said.

"It wouldn't have to be right away."

"But your friends are going soon, aren't they?"

"Tomorrow, as a matter of fact. But we could go, you know, anytime at all. If you wanted."

"As a matter of fact," he said, deliberately, "I'm going to have to take a small trip. More than a small trip, actually. I expect to be gone for two weeks, perhaps as long as a month."

"When?"

"I planned to leave the day after tomorrow. I hadn't told you because I'd been hoping something might come up to make me postpone it, but nothing has."

"Where do you have to go?"

"Washington."

"I could come with you. I might even be helpful. I can run errands, do research. And stay out of your way when you're busy."

"You tempt me. But it wouldn't work."

"Oh."

He took her hand. "An idea occurs to me. Why don't you go to the commune with your friends? The Land People? Go with your friends to the Land People."

"I don't want to go without you, Miles. I—"

"Let me finish. You go with them. I'll go to Washington. I'll take care of my business as quickly as I possibly can. I'll know you're at a good place, which will put my mind at ease and thus make the work go faster. Perhaps I'll be done sooner than I think.

In any case, I won't be more than a month. As soon as I've finished I'll find these Land People. If you've discovered you loathe it there, we'll leave. If you like it, we'll see how it suits us. The two of us, together."

Her eyes said, *Do you mean it? All of it?*

His said, *Yes.*

Her face glowed and he kissed her, and his passion surprised him as it had done so often lately. "Oh, let's make this the best ever," she said, fitting her body to his. "How can I go a month without you? God."

She asked the same question afterward, as she was drifting off to sleep.

"Oh, a week with the Land People and you'll forget me."

"I'll always love you, Miles. Always."

Will you, Jocelyn?

A fragment of dream awakened him. He was at an amusement-park shooting gallery, rifle in hand. Heads passed by, not the usual two-dimensional targets, but genuine heads, disembodied but nonetheless alive. Clyde Farrar, Jr., Burton Weldon, J. Lowell Drury, Emil Karnofsky, Willie Jackson, Royal Carter—an endless parade of the heads of those he had killed.

And, with no will of his own involved, he kept working the trigger, kept sending bullets into those heads. And each head turned into Jocelyn as he killed it, and each dying Jocelyn head fastened tortured eyes upon him, and yet he kept on working the trigger, kept turning head after head into Jocelyn.

He broke himself out of the dream. When his heart rate slowed, he turned to her, irrationally anxious that something had happened to her during his dream. But she slept peacefully on her side, one leg drawn up and bent at the knee. She was clutching her pillow in her sleep.

Karnofsky, too, had clutched his pillow.

She left in the afternoon, in a car with two boys and two girls. Dorn remembered them vaguely from the party. She took very little with her. Some clothing, and she would stop on the way to collect Vertigo. Her other clothing remained in Dorn's closet, her books on his shelves, her radio on his kitchen table.

After the car was gone, and after he had given himself up to a few minutes of weeping, Dorn reviewed his performance. As far as he could determine, she had not the slightest suspicion that she would never see him again.

FOURTEEN

In Washington he took a room

in a decent but no longer fashionable hotel. His room was on a high floor and he could see quite a bit of Washington from his window. He rarely availed himself of the view.

One of the first places he went in Washington was a chain drugstore, where he purchased a legal-sized pad of ruled yellow paper and several ball-point pens. He returned with his purchases to his room. There was a small writing desk. He seated himself at it, pen in hand, and stared for several minutes at the blank pad of paper.

Then he began to write.

My Jocelyn,

You hold in your hand a letter from a man you now know as the author of a heinous crime. Writing these lines, I ache at the thought of what you must now think of me. You must wonder how you could possibly have loved me. You must recoil at the realization that there was so much about me you could not begin to know.

And yet you knew me, Jocelyn, as no one had ever known me before.

Jocelyn, you know nothing of the man I have been or even of the man I am. Jocelyn, I first killed a man when I was seventeen years old. I killed him because he was a Serb and I was a Croat. At the time this seemed sufficient reason. By the time I was your age, Jocelyn, I literally could not count the men I had killed. I did not know their number.

109

He filled page after page in his small neat cramped hand. The words flowed of their own accord, and it was all he could do to make the pen move fast enough to get them down. When they stopped he set the pen down on the desk top and closed his eyes. His forearm throbbed all the way to the elbow. He rubbed it idly with his left hand.

After a few moments he got to his feet. He did not read what he had written, nor did he sever the filled pages from the pad. He went to the massive old dresser and, with an effort, pulled it free from the wall. He lifted the carpet where the dresser had been and placed the entire pad of yellow paper beneath it, then carefully pressed the carpet tacks back into place. Finally he returned the dresser to its original position and left the room.

No day passed without this ritual being repeated. Once every day he would shove the dresser aside and take up the pad of paper. Then he would sit at the small desk and write for as long as he had words to put down. The words did not always flow freely. Sometimes he found himself staring at the page before him for ten or twenty or thirty minutes in an effort to sort out a thought and get a sentence in its proper order. One day he wrote three short paragraphs in no time at all, then stopped abruptly, through for the day. But however much he wrote and however long it took, each day the pad of paper went back beneath the carpet, and each day the dresser was replaced over it.

When he was not writing or sleeping he moved around downtown Washington. He took several tours. On a tour of the White House his group unexpectedly encountered the President, who was then emerging from a conference with someone. The President smiled and shook hands with several members of the tour group. He did not shake hands with Dorn.

The Washington Monument and the Lincoln Memorial were key attractions on the tours Dorn took. He visited both of them afterward, by himself. Standing close to the Washington Monument and dizzied by its height, he thought of its particular appropriateness, an absolute phallus raised in tribute to the Father of his Country.

After his visit to the Lincoln Memorial, he wrote these words on the pad of yellow paper:

Once, Jocelyn, I asked you a pair of questions. I asked you, first, whom most Americans regarded as their greatest president. Without hesitation you named Abraham Lincoln. Then I asked you who you thought was the greatest American president. You thought for a moment. "Lincoln," you said.

There was a man named Henry Clay who never became president, his hopes notwithstanding. For a period of thirty years Henry Clay prevented the Civil War from taking place. Almost single-handedly he drafted one compromise after another. He adhered to no particular principle and made himself roundly despised as a man without principles. But for him, the South would surely have seceded at a time when the North could have done little to prevent secession.

Of course the election of Lincoln made secession inevitable, and war in turn was an inevitable consequence of secession. I often wonder what would have happened if Abraham Lincoln had not been elected. Mechanical developments, such as the cotton gin, would have made slavery obsolescent as an institution in not too many years. Other causes of sectionalist rivalary might have smoothed themselves out in much the same fashion.

Perhaps not. But it hardly matters, because Abraham Lincoln was in fact elected, and the South did secede, and war followed. And the North won, and the Union was preserved.

I was at the Lincoln Memorial this morning. I looked into the marble eyes of the most sorrowful face I have ever seen. It struck me, looking into the fact of that deeply troubled man, that Booth's bullet was an unintentional kindness.

There is no memorial to Henry Clay. I asked you once if you had heard of him. You knew the name.

One night Dorn went to a rally of the New American Patriots. The speaker was James Danton Rhodine. At the entrance to the auditorium Dorn was searched by two well-built and neatly groomed young men. Both wore the now standard royal blue shirts and khaki trousers. They were very well-mannered, and smiled as they apologized for the necessity of searching the men and women who had come to hear Rhodine.

This had become standard practice at NAP rallies ever since an unsuccessful attempt on Rhodine's life a month earlier in

San Francisco. Dorn took it for granted that this attempt had been staged. He found it increasingly difficult to believe that genuine assassination attempts ever ended in failure. It seemed as unlikely as a politically prominent person's dying a natural death. Possible, to be sure, but not likely.

Dorn found himself paying very little attention to the speech. He amused himself at the onset by anticipating the words before they were uttered. This palled before much time had elapsed. Thereafter, he found himself paying more attention to the crowd and the Blueshirts than to Rhodine.

He remained until the address was over and left the hall with the sound of rhythmic applause ringing in his ears. He went back to his hotel and went to sleep.

Every night, every single night, dreams woke Dorn. These dreams were rarely confined to a single language. Characters would begin a sentence in Serbo-Croat and end it in English. Then another character would respond in German or Russian. Heretofore Dorn's dreams had always confined themselves to one language at a time.

He interpreted this new element as another sign of confusion and anxiety. It thus distressed him, as such signs must, but he could not regard it as surprising or as cause for special worry.

He rarely had a dream without Jocelyn in it. In many of the dreams she died, most often at his hands. These dreams were the worst.

He never tried to return to sleep after a dream had awakened him. Each time he would wait until calm returned. Then he would shower and shave and dress. Then he might read from a paperback anthology of English poetry. Or walk through the predawn streets. Or move the dresser and take up the pad of yellow paper and add another passage to his endless letter to Jocelyn.

He never once read over what he had written. Nor did he ever discard a page or cross out a line. There were times when he wanted to do this last, times when he felt he had made a point badly. But he had decided that everything must stand as written.

Today as I was walking back to my hotel a fire engine passed me, siren open. My first thought was of a policeman in

*Philadelphia who could not understand why people would throw
rocks and bottles at firemen fighting a fire.*

*I thought next of my hotel. It is an old building, and no doubt
would burn like a torch. I froze at the thought of this manuscript
burning. Not that it might be discovered in the rubble but that
it might simply turn into a cinder.*

*There would not be time to write all of this again, Jocelyn,
nor do I think it likely that I would have the heart to try. I
stood on the pavement and visualized a lifetime of work going
up in smoke. "The work of a lifetime." Those were the words
that came to mind.*

*And, however grandiose they seem, I would not change them.
Jocelyn, I am drowning in Washington. My whole life passes
before my eyes, takes its form on these sheets of lined yellow
paper.*

*Of course it was not this building, nor even a building very
near to this one. My manuscript was not even warm to the touch.*

One afternoon he bought a bag of bread crumbs and went to
a park to feed pigeons. He threw out the bread crumbs in huge
handfuls so that the birds would not have to fight over them.
But no matter how fast he scattered the crumbs, so many more
pigeons kept coming that there was not standing room for them
all. They shouldered one another aside, pecked at each other,
puffed themselves up.

He left the park as soon as the bag was empty, not waiting to
watch them finish the crumbs.

It occurred to him from time to time that his letter to Jocelyn
was similar to Penelope's shawl. The letter would never end, and
until it ended he would not do the deed which had brought him
to Washington. But Penelope had unraveled each night what she
had knitted during that day. Dorn did no unraveling.

One day he wrote:

*You are the only person whose judgment matters the slightest
to me. I have never loved anyone but you. No one else has
ever truly known me. No living person but you has ever known
me at all. I realize that it is not unusual for a man to care deeply
about the opinion that strangers hold of him. I cannot
understand why this is true. I know that it is not true of me.*

113

Perhaps I ought to be tempted by the thought that History will vindicate me. But in the first place I doubt that History's judgment will be kind, and in the seond place I do not care in the slightest whether it is. The Judgment of History! The phrase itself is a joke, a contradiction in terms. History has no judgment. History is all blind men and elephants. Not a one of us, Jocelyn, knows much more than a very little about the peripheral facts of our own small lives. Yet History, removed in time and place, presumes to judge. The perspective of History is that special perspective afforded by a glance through the wrong end of a telescope. No man lives in History. Death is absolute.

Shall I then fear Death? I can only say that I do not. I have lived too long, Jocelyn, and to too little purpose. I find nothing very awful in the prospect of ceasing to be.

And yet. And yet one fear gnaws at me, Jocelyn. It eats at me like cancer. And that is the fear that you will hate me.

Before I met you, Jocelyn, no action of mine ever stemmed from a selfless purpose. Since then everything I have done has grown out of love for you. So I write these lines, these endless lines, to you. To gain your understanding. To win your forgiveness. To keep your love. You are my afterlife, Jocelyn. Your love is my Heaven, its absence all I need of Hell.

He stopped and reread the last paragraph, knowing that Penelope's shawl was complete. He had finished. Whatever could be said was said, whatever had been omitted would remain eternally unsaid. All that remained was to sign his name.

And yet, and yet.

His head ached, his forearm throbbed, his fingers were stiff. Aloud he said, "No, no," and the words turned into a low and agonizing groan.

He picked up the pen and wrote one final paragraph. He could not see the words as he wrote them. The tears flowed freely from his eyes and he did not even attempt to halt them.

Nor did he reread the final paragraph. He wrote his name, *Miles Dorn*, beneath the last line.

Later, when he had composed himself, he returned the pad of yellow paper to its place beneath the carpet. For the last time he pushed the dresser in place over it. Then he went downstairs and found a telephone.

FIFTEEN

"I anticipate your question,"

Heidigger said. "The room is electronically clean. It always is, and yet you always ask, so I tell you in advance."

"How can you be certain?"

"Two clever devices. One of them somehow senses the presence of any electronic ears. Please do not ask me how as I have not the slightest idea. The process was once explained to me, leaving me as ignorant as before. The other device is predicated on the assumption that the first device is not foolproof. It emits a signal that renders any electronic surveillance of the premises quite ineffective. Of course whenever the first device tells me someone is listening, I immediately change my room. I tell the desk that my room is too large, or too small, or that I saw a mouse in a corner. They are always quite obliging in such matters."

"Does that happen often?"

"More often than you might think. Not because the surveillance was designed with me in mind, however. I have never had cause to suspect that to be the case. But there is so much of this bugging going on, Miles, and it would be an embarrassment to be taped quite by mistake, would it not?" Heidigger laughed happily at the thought. "But the devil with all that. The devil with machines. I find it difficult to think in terms of machines. I use them, one cannot but use them, but I have small faith it them. Machines cancel each other out. In the final analysis, it is men who must make the difference."

"I agree."

"Men like you, Miles Dorn. Let me look at you." Heidigger struck a pose, chin in hand, brow quizzical. "I do believe all of this has changed you, you know. Which I do not find surprising in the least. Your achievements have made an extraordinary impression in high places. Which is as it should be. They have been extraordinary achievements."

"You're kind to say so."

"How could I say otherwise? Five prominent men, five men in the public eye. That one lived is nothing. He could be no less a threat if he had died. Nor is it more than an interesting footnote that you only killed three of the four who died. One takes help where one finds it, eh?"

I killed three, Eric. But not the three you think. You credit me with Walter Isaac James, a death with which I had nothing whatsoever to do. And deny me the credit for Emil Karnofsky.

"I brought what you asked for, Miles." He took a vial of pills from an inside jacket pocket. "Two dozen of them. I was surprised you did not already have some of your own."

"For years I never moved without at least one on my person."

"I still don't."

"And then after my retirement I kept a bottle of them always at hand. A vestigial remnant. It became increasingly clear that I would have no call for them in my new life, until one day I found them in the medicine cabinet and had momentary trouble remembering what they were. It struck me that the faint possibility of ingesting one accidentally far outweighed my possible future need for them. I flushed them down the toilet."

Eric, I itch to tell you about Karnofsky. Because I know damned well you checked. Those casual questions. How had I planned to enter the building? And then you sent someone to make quite certain I had visited that psychiatrist, just as you sent someone else to make sure I had been in my room in New Orleans when Karnofsky died. I would love to tell you all this, Eric. I would love to see your face.

"Make sure they're what you want."

Dorn opened the vial, took a capsule between thumb and forefingers.

"Plastic," Heidigger said. "Nonsoluble in mouth or stomach. It must be crushed between the teeth."

"Cyanide?"

"In English, cyanide. In Japanese, sayonara. The effects are virtually instantaneous."

"Yes."

"And not dreadfully unpleasant, or so I am told. But there is a dearth of firsthand evidence on the subject. No one ever returns to testify."

"Which is the object."

"That no one testify? To be sure. You want them for your men, I imagine. Remember, though, that the likelihood of their

116

using them is remote. You or I might recognize when self-destruction is the only alternative. Even the most fanatic of amateurs usually flinch at it. It is child's play to persuade a true believer to undertake a mission where his chance of survival is infinitesimal. Yet the same man will so often balk at killing himself."

"At least they'll have the option. Whether they exercise it or not, their trail won't lead back to me."

"You're very sure of this?"

"I am." He suddenly smiled. "Nevertheless, one of those capsules is for me, Eric. I will not be caught. But if by any chance I am—"

"I understand."

Do you, Eric? And do you think I do not realize that I would not outlive Henry M. Theodore by a day? That some man of yours would gun me down before any trail could possibly turn me up? To think otherwise would be to think you a fool. You are not a fool, Eric. You are not quite as brilliant as you think, but you are by no means a fool.

"It is all in order, then."

"Completely so."

"Would it be in order to ask the day?"

"Why not? Today. A matter of hours."

"Again you surprise me, Miles."

"At three o'clock the President and his worthy and respected associate, the Vice-President, will leave the White House in the presidential limousine. At three-thirty the President will address a joint session of congress on the most recent development at the Paris peace talks. The development, rumor has it, is that there has been no development."

"Nor will there be."

"There will, however, be a development before that joint session of congress opens. A development of sufficient moment to cancel that session, I would think."

"I too would think so." Heidigger whistled tonelessly. "I think at once of the security, the fantastic security. But of course you have already considered this."

"Of course."

"And you have made a plan that penetrates all of this security."

"Of course."

"And that leaves no room for doubt that this horrible act is

117

the work not of a deranged soul but of a heartless and soulless conspiracy."

"Of course."

Eric, I want to tell you about Karnofsky. God, do I want to tell you about Karnofsky!

He listened as Heidigger told him that no other man could do what he, Miles Dorn, was doing. And he thought that this was very likely true, and in ways Heidigger did not imagine.

And then he broke into a sentence.

"Eric, is that the device you were talking about? The electronic wonder?"

"Where?"

"There—"

And even as the head was turning, his hand was in motion, reaching for the back of the neck, reaching, making the grab precisely. Intercepting the flow of blood to the brain, cutting it off neatly, neatly.

He caught Heidigger as he fell, eased him gently to the floor. He knelt beside the man. The thick glasses had slipped down on the nose. He replaced them, his hands gentle.

"And how I wanted to tell you about Karnofsky, Eric," he said aloud. "Childish of me, eh? But you shall not hear it, old friend. It is the least I can do for you, is it not? To grant you the bliss of dying in ignorance."

He uncapped the little vial, let a capsule role out onto the palm of his hand. He pried open Heidigger's jaw.

"They will even bury you with your gold teeth, Eric. This is America. A free country."

He lodged the capsule between Heidigger's teeth. He put one hand on the bald head, one on the underside of the chin. He turned his own head aside and pressed his hands toward one another.

There was a faint, almost undetectable odor of almonds.

"My old friend," he said, looking down at the corpse. "My oldest, dearest friend." He spoke the words several times over, and meant them. But he spoke with no tears in his eyes and not a trace of sorrow in his voice.

A careful search of the room revealed no gun. He had expected that Heidigger would have a gun on his person or in his luggage

118

and was mildly annoyed that this was not the case. This was inconvenient, but his schedule allowed for the inconvenience.

He found a coded address and memorandum book in Heidigger's pocket. He was at first inclined to leave it on the corpse, then changed his mind and put it in his own pocket. In its place he left a letter in his own hand to Heidigger, giving a version of his plan for terminating Case Six. He had prepared the letter in the most difficult code he was able to devise, an elaborate cipher based on a Serbo-Croat key word. He doubted that any decent government cryptographer would have any appreciable degree of difficulty cracking the code.

He also found, among Heidigger's effects, a packet of pornographic photos of an interracial couple and an electrical masturbatory device. He laughed aloud, and returned these to the drawer in which he had found them.

When he was quite through, he removed from one of his own pockets a thick sheaf of folded sheets of lined yellow paper. His letter to Jocelyn.

He checked his watch. There was time. Even with the necessity of obtaining a gun, there was time.

He sat down in an armchair and read the letter from its beginning to its end.

Here are parts of what he read:

My Jocelyn,
   You hold in your hand a letter from a man you now know as the author of a heinous crime. . . .

Do you remember the day my house stank of Turkish cigarettes? The following day I traveled to Tampa to meet a man named Eric Heidigger. He wanted to employ me in the only profession I have ever practiced, that of assassination. He wanted me to kill the following men. . . .

What I could not get out of my head, Jocelyn, was not that the plan was outrageous but that it was so eminently feasible. His analysis of the state of the country was weighted, but not much so. And it seemed to me that fulfillment of the plan did not hinge upon its execution. I looked at the country and saw it all beginning to happen. . . .

*Why, you might wonder, did I not report this to the authorities?
I did consider this. But what precisely did I have to report?
Some fanciful plan concocted by some not-to-be-found Eric
Heidigger? And to whom would I make my report? Suppose I
poured all this into an ear that already knew. And approved. . . .*

*You will wonder, then, why I felt compelled to take any
action at all. Perhaps you will recall my own advice to you. To
avoid involvement. To survive.*

*But I could not survive in any event. From the moment I
met with Heidigger in Tampa my own death was inevitable.
It was only a matter of time. If I did not take Heidigger's
assignment, I would in turn become someone else's assignment.
If I were not part of his solution, I became part of his problem.
My knowledge of the plan was only acceptable so long as I was
part of that plan.*

*I might have tried flight. Halfway across the world the
trouble in killing me would be greater than the hazard I would
present. But I made a promise to myself, Jocelyn. I swore
not to commit suicide, and I swore not to leave the country.
You might be interested in the source of this oath. . . .*

*Do you remember Eichmann's plea in Jerusalem? I still find
it amusing. That he was only following orders. That he was given
a job to do, and that the job would be performed by someone
else if he refused it. And that he thus resolved to carry it out
as well as he possibly could.*

*I, too, was confronted with a job that would be done by
someone else should I refuse to undertake it. Heidigger liked
to flatter me that no man alive could do the task as well as I.
But any number of men could and would have done it, one way
or another. I have told you that, from the time of that meeting
in Tampa, my death was a foregone conclusion. But so were
the deaths of the men on that list. I could not possibly have
prevented this. . . .*

*One thing I could do. In one respect I was in fact unique.
I knew Heidigger's plan. I was a part of Heidigger's plan.*

And I was opposed to it.

*Thus I was in an extraordinary position, that of a fifth column
within a fifth column. A precarious position at that, because*

I had to do the job given to me while modifying its results in certain important but not readily detectable ways. . . .

I could easily have made Drury's murder the act of a conspiracy, or at least the act of a rational leftist assassin. But by taking pains to cloak Burton Weldon in the trappings of madness . . .

With Karnofsky, I arranged that both Heidigger and most of the public would see the murder as the result of a burglary. But among the more knowledgeable labor leaders there would be some suspicion, some slight feeling . . .

You thought Guthrie ought to die. At the time I supplied a reason or two why he should not. I did not mention the one that moved me to keep him alive.

It was simply this. Racism will be a factor in American politics for many years, if not indeed forever. And there must be a voice that speaks for this racist opinion. Such a voice may be dangerous or innocuous. Guthrie was not dangerous because he never possessed the potential for national success. Heidigger knew this. Thus, in his profoundly offensive way, he constituted a safeguard to American democracy.

Imagine, Jocelyn, how astonished he himself would be to know this!

But I was willing to see him dead. I hoped it would work out as it did, but the tolerance in dealing with explosives . . . In any case, I felt the death of Willie Jackson would tend to separate moderate blacks from the bomb throwers. Whether it had this effect I could not say. One small event among so many . . .

. . . and thus decided not to kill James. It will never be possible for me to know how much of this stemmed from reason and how much I owe to the fact of our having become lovers. I am sure the latter had some effect. . . . But reason was partly responsible, too. You see, Jocelyn, I felt it was important that James live. I felt the role he played was a positive one, a more valuable one than that played by any of the others.

But how can I possibly make you understand, how can I dare to expect you to understand, that the deaths of innocent

121

persons affect me not at all? How can I convince you of this without at once convincing you that I am a monster?

Nor, on reflection, is the statement wholly true. I am moved by human death, but no more and in no hugely different way than I am by the death of any animal. That baby bird that Vertigo killed, for one example. The chicken we ate for dinner our last night together, for another. I grieve as deeply for that chicken as I do for J. Lowell Drury. I cannot see (and I suspect the fault is mine) any difference between taking the one life and the other. But this does not move me to vegetarianism, either. . . .

And so I made the mistake of forgetting who I am. I am a killer. For a moment I thought I was God, and that James would live because I had decided that he should live. But my failing to kill him did not immunize him from death at another's hands.

I learned from this. I learned something I had already known, but one only learns what one already knows. What I learned was that these events would come to pass not only without my participation but also without the movement of which Heidigger and I were a part. Acts grow out of their time. And so I killed P. J. O'Dowd, not because it mattered to me or to Heidigger that he live or die, but lest someone else kill him in a more damaging way. . . .

I have been over this so many times. There is a danger on the right, and every move the left makes strengthens it. Rhodine himself hardly matters. Remove him and another would take his place.

I am just one man, Jocelyn. I am trying to do what I can to make this country as fit as it can be for you to live in. But I am just one man. I do not know how much effect I can have.

The center holds the only answer. If there is an answer.

Again and again I find myself blinking back thoughts of the unthinkable. That the answer is that there is no answer. But I must go on acting as if I do not believe this to be true. . . .

And the last page:

And yet. And yet one fear gnaws at me, Jocelyn. It eats at me like cancer. And that is the fear that you will hate me.

Before I met you, Jocelyn, no action of mine ever stemmed from a selfless purpose. Since then, everything I have done has grown out of love for you. So I write these lines, these endless lines, to you. To gain your understanding. To win your forgiveness. To keep your love. You are my afterlife, Jocelyn. Your love is my Heaven, its absence all I need of Hell. . . .

And the last paragraph:

Oh, my darling, my love, my life. Love of you made me selfless. Now it makes me self-sacrificing, because for it I must give up the only thing I want. For I cannot possibly send this letter to you, Jocelyn, my Jocelyn. I write to you knowing you must be spared my words. I cannot burden you with this knowledge. I cannot permit you to share it. You will be questioned at great length. You must know no more than I have already shown you. And what I have shielded from the world, I thus must shield from you as well. You said you would always love me, Jocelyn, and were it true I could bear anything. But you will know of me what the world knows, not what I have written here. For your sake, Jocelyn. But I cannot bear it, I cannot bear it, and something dies now within me.

Miles Dorn

He shed no tears while he read the letter. He would never weep again. The part of him that wept no longer existed. He read the letter dry-eyed all the way through to the signature. Then he burned it, page by page, in Heidigger's wastebasket. He watched as each piece of yellow paper in its turn caught fire and flamed.

When the last sheet was consumed he stirred the ashes thoroughly. Then, although he knew that the most painstaking laboratory work in the world could not reconstitute those pages, he nevertheless took the wastebasket into the bathroom and flushed the ashes down the toilet. Already the air conditioner was beginning to clear the smoke from the room.

He left all of the cyanide capsules but one at Heidigger's side. He let himself out of the room, hung the *Do Not Disturb* sign on the knob. The inside lock was the sort he could engage from the outside. He turned the bolt, put the room key in his pocket, and left.

SIXTEEN

His body moved, acted, performed. It knew its role and did what it was supposed to do. His mind was only peripherally aware of what was going on. For the most part his thoughts wandered in space and time, playing with words and phrases, listening to voices other than his own.

Henry Michael Theodore. Vice-President, United States of America. An intuitive political amateur with an instinctive appreciation of centrist and right-centrist anxieties. A refined demagogue. . . .

His suit jacket hid the gun stuck in the waistband of his trousers. The patrolman whose service revolver it was would never miss it. He was dead now, in an alley, his neck expertly broken. Dorn had expected Heidigger to have a gun in his room. Finding none, he had not wanted to waste time devising a clever way to get one.

The easiest way was the best. Policemen carried guns. Dead policemen have no need for them. A policeman going to the aid of an apparent mugging victim does not expect that mugging victim to reach up suddenly and break his neck. No amount of training can prepare a policeman for such an eventuality.

(*"I voted for the President in the last election. You know who a lot of cops voted for? . . . Guthrie. . . . You know who they're talking about more and more? . . . Your man Rhodine . . . You know who else I like is Theodore. Of course, he hasn't got Rhodine's style. But I like what he's got to say."*)

It was so easy. That was perhaps the most frightening thing about it, that it had all been so absurdly easy from beginning to end. Even the genuinely complicated parts were difficult only in their conception, not in their execution.

. . . . Romanian ancestry, original name Teodorescu. Theodore's moderate right-centrist stance and his extraordinary success at focusing white middle-class discontent make his termination a quintessential ingredient in movement policy. . . .

124

But didn't they know how easy it was? Didn't everyone know? It seemed to him that Dallas should have taught them that much. Not the assassination of Kennedy. But the assassination of Oswald, when one man with a gun walked through everyone and committed the world's first televised murder.

One man with a gun.

(*"Sweet old Theodorable. . . . Oh, God, I hate that man. When I see him on television I want to kick the screen in. Somebody ought to put a bullet through that head of his. . . . That man is tearing the country apart, and the more he does it the more the idiots applaud. I think he's a dangerous man."*)

What was Jocelyn doing now? She was at the commune with the Land People, and it bothered him that he could not picture the place in his mind. Perhaps she was working in the garden. Or putting up preserves for the winter. Or talking with someone, or sitting around high on marijuana. Or making love.

(*"I'll always love you, Miles. Always."*)

Will you, Jocelyn? Will you? I am going to believe that you will. Permit me a little self-deception. Permit me to believe this. I will not have to believe it for very much longer.

. . . . It should be scheduled at least one and no more than three months after Guthrie's termination. Terminal thrust must be unmistakably via large-scale leftist conspiracy. Involvement should extend to both black and white radicals. . . .

One man with a gun. One man with a gun, in the right place at the right time. One man with a gun at the Capitol steps as the presidential limousine approaches.

N.B.—It is imperative that the terminal cover be wholly opaque. Not only must there be no official or unofficial suspicion of movement involvement, but there can be no evidence of any involvement that is not absolutely identifiable as leftist and/or black.

One man with a gun. In one pocket, a key to a room at the Holiday Inn. In another pocket, Heidigger's coded address and memorandum book. In his mouth, tucked in a cheek, a plastic-coated capsule filled with cyanide. A capsule that would not dissolve in the mouth or in the stomach. A capsule that had to be crushed between the teeth.

(*"I will not kill myself. I will not leave the country."*)

One man with a gun. One man with a gun in the waistband of his trousers, moving forward as the presidential limousine disgorges its contents. One man with a gun in his hand, moving through the crowd like a ghost through walls.

("But didn't they know how easy it was? Didn't everyone know?")

One man with a gun. One man with a gun in his hand.

("If you are not part of the solution, then you must be part of the problem.")

One man emptying that gun point-blank into the chest of the President of the United States.

And turning even as the last bullet hit home. Turning, empty gun in hand, cyanide capsule still tucked between cheek and gum.

("I will not kill myself.")

One man with a gun, turning to point the empty gun at the Vice-President of the United States.

("Sweet old Theodorable . . . .")

One man with a gun. One man with an empty gun that no one else knew was empty. One man with a gun pointed at the Vice-President of the United States while Secret Service men threw themselves over the president's body.

Fools! Do you think I could miss?

One man with a gun, welcoming the bullets that pierced his flesh.

It took so long to die. *La grande mort.* He fell so slowly. Whoever would have thought the ground would be so far away? The ground was miles away. *(Miles from Croatia.)* The feel of the plastic capsule against his gum. *(I will not—)* How odd it felt, this business of dying.

I die in your arms, Jocelyn.

"I'll always love you, Miles. Always."

Jocelyn—